Simply Provocative

Simply Provocative

A Spruce Creek Romance

Sharon Burgess

A Russian Hill Press Book
United States • United Kingdom • Australia

 Russian Hill Press

The publisher is not responsible for websites (or their content) that are not owned by the publisher.

Copyright © 2016 by Sharon F. Svitak

Cover Design: Christine McCall
Cover Photograph: Paul McGowan
Cover Silhouette: Craig Toron
Editor: Kristi Cook

LCCN: 2016939529
ISBN: 978-0-9911973-5-4

DEDICATION

For every married couple in the world whose relationship has come to the brink of destruction, and for those who have managed to reconcile and go on to have a stronger union.

ACKNOWLEDGMENTS

Special thanks to my critique partners, Judy and Nate; to my beta readers, Alice, Julie, and Kim; to my line editor and proofreader, Violet Moore; and to all my supporters at the California Writers Club and the San Francisco Area Chapter, Romance Writers of America; and finally, saving the best until last, everlasting gratitude to my incredible editor, Kristi Cook.

Without all of you this book would never have made it into print.

ONE

JESSIE JOLTED WHEN, AS THE CAR ROLLED TO A stop, her brother tapped her shoulder. "Wake up, Sis, we're here."

Shivering, she hugged her jacket close to her body to ward off the late March chill. She inhaled the alpine air and sighed with pleasure. "I wasn't asleep, Jerm—simply resting my eyes."

"Jessica Walker Whitaker, stop calling me Jerm." He spoke sternly. "I'm a grown man, not a toddler." His face sported a mischievous grin, just like when he was a kid. "My name is Jeremy."

"Okay, I won't do it again . . . Jerm," she responded with the hint of a smirk. *It was fun to bicker with siblings. How she'd missed her brothers while she was away.*

She looked toward the front door of her little

gray house with its small sheltered porch. Unexpectedly, her husband stepped out onto that tiny stoop. His rugged good looks took her breath away—broad shoulders, straight spine, wind-blown ash brown hair falling into his eyes and resting on his collar—the *Marlboro* man in person. But she refused to let his good looks overwhelm her again as they once had done.

"Matthew Andrew Whitaker, what are you doing here?" She snapped as she climbed the steps, waving farewell to her brother before she entered her house. "Is this your idea of a joke?"

"What sort of greeting is that? Doesn't your husband deserve hello, how are you, good to see you?" His voice sounded warm and friendly in spite of her grouchy remark.

Why can't that man ever snap back?

She had no intention, however, of starting an argument her first day home, even if she was irritated to find him in her house. "You still haven't answered my question. Why are you here?"

"I came to get the house ready." He rattled off a long litany of preparations. "I've turned on the water, fueled the propane tank, put fresh linens on your bed, and stocked the kitchen and the freezer. I got rid of all the cobwebs in the corners, cleared out the squirrels nested in the chimney, and laid a fire. Doesn't that earn me a friendly greeting?"

"Sorry, I'm travel weary and I'm cranky. I don't want to spar with you. I just want to shed my clothes, take a shower, and go to bed."

"Hey, I'm in favor of that. I'll be glad to help."

"Matt, don't start. I'm too tired to fence with you."

"Jess, the last thing I wish is to engage in verbal combat. You're my wife. I love you. And in spite of your current confused state, I'm convinced you love me too. Come here, sweetheart."

Matt pulled her into a close hug. She tensed for a second, and then she relaxed into his embrace. "You're right, I do love you. But I did a lot of reflecting while I was away. And while this isn't the time to discuss our situation, I have to be up front. I don't think our marriage can survive our irreconcilable differences."

"We don't have irreconcilable differences. We have difficult choices," he responded, following her from the front of the house into the bedroom.

"Maybe," Jessie said.

"As long as we love each other, we can work through them. You'll come to realize I'm right."

Her husband was the eternal optimist. He would work forever to resolve their issues if that's how long a resolution took. But he would be disappointed. Their issues would never be resolved. "Matthew, I'm not ready to get into this conversation. I want you to leave now. Go home."

"Look, you'll feel better after a shower and a change of clothes." He pushed her toward the bathroom. "I'll put a match to the fire and fix you a light supper and a glass of wine while you bathe. Go."

She was aware he expected her capitulation, even if it wouldn't last long. She intended to perk up after her shower and come back with all guns blazing. But for now, she'd move in the direction he pointed her and let Matt have this minor victory. *It wasn't as if I could do anything else.*

After her shower, Jessie, clad in pajamas and a robe, came into the dining area. Matt had lit a fire in the front parlor and returned to the kitchen to fix a salad. She moaned at the aroma of her favorite casserole and her stomach growled. She knew Matt had heard.

Grinning, he escorted her to the breakfast nook. When the salad was tossed, he pulled the casserole from the microwave, dished up the food, and put the plates on the table. It looked as if she and Matt would eat together. She bit her tongue to avoid nagging. Truth was she would prefer to dine alone.

When they finished the meal, she followed Matt into the parlor and settled onto the couch in front of the fire. Matt turned on her CD player to easy listening and brought her another glass of wine.

Jessie snuggled under a lap blanket soaking up the comfort of being home, well fed, and enjoying the music. She stretched out on the couch and closed her eyes—just for a moment.

As Matt moved about preparing supper while Jessie was taking her shower, he chuckled remembering the look of dismay on Jessie's face when she'd arrived. She hadn't expected to see him waiting on her porch. Since they'd been apart for months, he'd anticipated resistance to his presence, but their marriage was too fragile for him to wait patiently for her to seek him out. He was determined they wouldn't end up in a divorce. That's what her letters home had hinted.

He was disturbed by some of the changes in her appearance. She'd lost weight and her fair skin was too pale by far. She'd cut her dark brown hair. He would miss running his hands through her long, silky tresses, but the new hairstyle wasn't unattractive. His greatest concern was that Jessica looked exhausted. He intended to do something about her frail appearance, starting with a good meal.

His housekeeper, Consuela, had prepared Jessie's favorite enchilada casserole. The food was cooked but needed to be reheated in the microwave. In the breakfast nook, he set the small surface with dishes and flatware. He'd made a point of placing flowers at the center of the little table.

By the time Jessie came into the kitchen, Matt had finished tossing the salad and pulled the casserole from the microwave. He knew he was presenting her with a *fait accompli*. She would have no choice but to have supper with him. The look on her face told him she was aware of his maneuver. And Jessica hated to be maneuvered.

Before she was able to protest, he served the casserole directly from the counter onto their plates. He slipped into the chair across from her and poured her a glass of wine, then handed her the salad. He started to eat before she could banish him.

"So, did you accomplish everything you wanted while in New York City?" he asked after swallowing his first bite. "Where did you go and what did you see? I know you can't have been working and studying every single minute."

"I did spend a huge amount of time going to class and working," Jessie replied, "but I visited the New York Public Library and the Museum of Modern Art. I saw a few Broadway shows and attended salons to network with authors and other illustrators."

He continued to ask questions, and Jessie told him about her stay. She also told him, "I'm just so happy to be back in Colorado. I missed the mountains, the small towns, and the western way of life. I missed my brothers."

He noticed Jessie didn't include him with the people she'd missed. But it didn't sound to him as if she would be returning to New York City any time soon.

In the kitchen he cleared the table, rinsed the dishes, and loaded the dishwasher. *I'll sweep her off her feet with kindness.*

When he went into the living room, he saw she'd dozed. Exhausted from her trip and with her internal time clock still set on East Coast time, plus two glasses of wine, it was no wonder she'd fallen asleep.

After turning down the bed, he picked her up and carried her into the bedroom. He inhaled the citrusy smell of her freshly washed hair and remembered their early years together. He wondered how those years had slipped away. Jessie cuddled into his arms and nestled her nose into his throat, proving to him she was indeed asleep. She was too prickly to snuggle if she'd been awake.

Untangling her arms from his neck, he gently placed her onto the bed, slipped her out of her robe, and covered her with blankets. Then he went through the house turning out lights, banking the fire, and locking the doors.

When he returned to the bedroom he debated with himself, but not for long. What the hell, she was his wife, and she'd been away a long time. Stripping off his clothes, he climbed into bed and enjoyed the sensation of sleeping next to his love.

JESSICA'S FIRST AWARENESS WAS THE SOUND OF a bird singing outside the window, the sweet trills bringing her to wakefulness. Morning light brightened the bedroom. Inexplicably happy, she stretched, feeling warm and comfortable.

Then she realized her naked husband was spooned around her, his arm resting across her stomach, an early morning hard-on pressed against her behind. She froze as she tried to recall the night before. She remembered supper and settling onto the couch in the living room, but nothing after that. *I must have fallen asleep . . . is that what happened?* She had no recollection of either climbing in bed with him or encouraging him to join her. In fact, memory insisted the last place she'd been awake was stretched out on the sofa after dinner.

With no intention of waking him, she carefully lifted the arm encircling her and tried to roll away. The arm tightened.

"I have you now, and I'm not going to let you go," he whispered in her ear.

She struggled against him, and Matt released her at once. *Thank God, he would never force himself on me, even though we're married.* She jumped out of bed and moved out of his reach.

"Come back to bed. We can at least cuddle."

"Matt, you're naked. We won't stop at cuddling, and you know that."

"Come on, honey, I've had a long dry spell."

Jessie felt a pang of guilt. She was confident Matt had remained faithful to her for the year she'd been gone. And even though she thought their marriage was going to fail, she'd remained faithful to him too. But she knew she mustn't let him seduce her. The problem was that they envisioned completely different futures. He wanted a big family. She wasn't prepared to have any children. This could never be reconciled, no matter how hard they tried.

Since there is so much at stake—my very identity—it means I shouldn't look at his incredible body. I can't risk the temptation.

A big man, even bigger than her brothers, his face was craggy and weathered as a result of working outdoors. He had some facial hair, as if he were growing a beard. His sun-streaked hair was always in need of a trim. He had a wicked smile that made her putty in his hands. She'd loved him since high school, but she wasn't convinced she could remain married to him.

"Go shower," she said turning away. "I'll fix breakfast and then you must go. We aren't going to play house."

She watched as Matt rolled over and pulled a pillow over his head. "You're a heartless wench," he mumbled.

Laughing at his comeback, Jessie headed for the kitchen. A mess of eggs, bacon, and hash browns would restore his good mood. But before anything else, they both needed coffee. She plugged in the Keurig, spun the coffee carousel, and then selected her favorite. *How considerate of Matt to make certain my first choice was at hand.* With her coffee made first, she set up Matt's. She would brew his when the shower shut off.

When he walked into the kitchen, she handed him his coffee. The scrambled eggs were firm and the bacon sizzled. She'd added bell pepper and onions to the potatoes, and now everything was ready to come off the stove. *He'd better not complain about breakfast.*

They both shoveled in food, neither one inclined to interrupt eating the first meal of the day with chatter. They weren't morning conversationalists until after caffeine hit the brain.

When they'd blunted the edge of their hunger and each was sipping a second cup of coffee, Matt said, "Jordan and his new bride, Kathleen, plan to stop by before lunch."

"What's she like?" Jessie asked.

"Kat's petite, but feisty," Matt said with a grin. "I watched her vaccinate my goats without taking a break. Between her and Jordan, they inoculated all two hundred animals in just over an hour. She doesn't put up with shit from him. She accused him of treating her like a pampered pet and jumped on his case."

"I never thought the day would come when my brother would move beyond his distrust of women and find a wife. I still can't believe he's married."

Matt described the wedding. "The ceremony was small and informal because they married in the dead of winter. Jeremy, Torrey, and I were the only ones present, and . . ."

"How is Torrey?" Jessica interrupted. "I can't wait to see her." He'd started to reply to her question when she stopped him. "Go ahead," she said. "Finish your story about the wedding."

"Even Kat's family couldn't come for the ceremony because of the road conditions," Matt continued. "But your brother and Kat plan to have a church rite with a big reception in the fall. That's why they weren't too disappointed you couldn't get home."

"I look forward to meeting her. She must be quite a woman if she could lasso Jordan."

"I think I'll hang around. I want to see your reaction when you meet her."

"Matt, go home or go away. You're not moving in with me."

"Of course not, I have a ranch to run. But it won't hurt anything if I stay for a few hours until Jordan and Kat arrive. Besides, you can unpack. I can put your suitcases away and start a load of laundry for you."

"Matt, you're impossible. You may stay until they get here, but I'll do my own laundry, thank you."

They worked in companionable silence. They'd been sweethearts since high school but not married until she was twenty-seven when Jeremy left for college. Even so, they knew each other's moods and methods. Jessie, moving a load from the washer to the dryer, heard a knock.

"I'll get it," Matt called out.

He opened the door and urged Jordan and Kat to come in out of the cold. Jordan grinned at his brother-in-law. "Matt, you dog. You got Jessie to let you move in."

"I heard that," Jessie called from the laundry room. "Matt has not mooved in. He's just here helping out."

"Jessie, get out here and meet my wife," her

brother, Jordan, demanded.

When Jessie walked into the living room, she couldn't believe her eyes. Her brother had robbed the proverbial cradle. The girl in front of her was petite as Matt had said, but she also sported freckles, wore her russet hair in braids, and couldn't be over eighteen.

Her new sister-in-law obviously read her mind. Stretching out her hand to Jessie she said, "Hi, I'm Kat, and I'm twenty-five."

"I'm sorry. Were my thoughts that obvious?"

Kat laughed. "You had dismay written all over your face. Don't feel badly. I'm accustomed to your reaction. I can't walk into a bar without being carded. And I'm hit on by high school boys all the time."

Jessie laughed. She liked her brother's wife. She ushered the couple into the living room and then turned to Matt. "I'll just see you out. Have a safe trip back to the ranch."

Matt left without argument, but at the door he whispered, "This battle isn't over—it has barely begun."

TWO

A WEEK HAD PASSED SINCE MATT HAD SEEN OR talked with Jessie. He scarcely slept and when he dozed off, he dreamed of her. He heard himself barking at the ranch hands. And if he dared, he would be snapping at Consuela. *How much longer could he hold out now that Jess was just down the mountain and not separated from him by half a continent?* He needed a plan.

Torrey Hansen, Jordan's clinic manager, knew Jessie better than anyone, including her brothers. Torrey had been her surrogate mother after Jolene Walker abandoned her family. Matt would enlist Torrey in his efforts to save his marriage.

Matt packed a small bag, hoping he would spend a night or two in Spruce Creek. He left word with Consuela that he was going to town and might not be back for a few days. He drove his Range Rover, identical to the one he had bought Jessie, up to the corrals where his foreman was at work. After leaving instructions with him for the hands, he headed into town.

The road out of the ranch was a combination of mud and ice. While the trip during late summer and early fall could be a beautiful drive, with views of blue spruce and aspen trees, it certainly wasn't a pleasure today. *Who could enjoy scenery while struggling to keep a truck on the road?* Matt decided he needed to get a grader in to scrape and level the surface and then dump a couple truckloads of gravel.

When he got to Spruce Creek, he pulled behind Jordan's clinic and left his Rover in the family/employee parking area. He came in through the back entrance and asked the first person he saw where he would find Torrey. When he located her, she was unpacking a box of vet supplies that had been delivered by FedEx. She hummed to herself as she sorted the supplies for stocking.

"Hi, Torrey, got a minute?"

She glanced up from the supplies and smiled. "For you, of course I do. Jordan and Kat are in the field today, so there's not much happening here at the clinic."

"Can I talk to you in private?"

Torrey rose, brushing off her hands on her pants. "Okay. We'll use Jordan's office." After closing the door behind her, she settled into the chair at Jordan's desk. "What's so private you don't want to talk out there?"

"You know my marriage is in trouble?" Matt said, leaning forward and putting his hand onto the desk.

"Honey, everybody in the county knows your marriage is in trouble. And none of us can understand why. You and Jess have been a couple since high school."

"I need your help to win Jess back. I need a plan," Matt declared. "You understand her better than anyone else in the world. I don't know what to do to salvage our relationship. She is so distant."

Torrey nodded. "First, you need to understand what Jess is feeling. Put yourself in her place. Determine what she is afraid of. Then, do whatever is necessary to remove that fear."

Matt started to interrupt, but Torrey cut him off. "Decide what you are willing to do to save your marriage. That's the bottom line."

"Well, she's convinced the ranch is too isolated for her to run a business," Matt said. "So I decided today, as I was mucking my way down the mountain, that I need to gravel the road. And I'm more than willing to do other things. She doesn't trust me, so I can't figure how to get her up to the ranch to see any changes I do make."

"Okay, Matt, here's the plan," Torrey said, tapping a finger on the desk. "May nineteenth is Jordan's birthday. Can you get all the changes in place by then?"

"Sure, that's over six weeks—more than enough time as long as we don't have a blizzard between now and then."

"You'll host a big birthday party at the ranch for Jordan. Jess will have to come up for that. In the meanwhile, you're going to court that girl."

"Court her? What do you mean?"

Torrey grinned. "Jess fell head over heels in love with you the day you two met. I know because she told me all about it. You never had to do anything to make her love you—she just did."

Matt nodded his agreement. He'd fallen for her in just the same way.

"Now you must win her heart again," Torrey continued. "You'll bring her flowers, buy her candy and perfume, and give her feminine impractical gifts, girlie things. You'll take her on a special date, dinner and dancing. I suggest the Brown Palace."

"I'm not certain such ploys will work. Jess still loves me. She's said so. She just doesn't want to stay married."

"Then you must make marriage to you the thing she wants most in the world."

Matt's eyes lit up in anticipation. He liked the idea of courting Jessie.

"Okay, Matt, there's your plan. Get to it!"

JESSICA WOKE IN A ROTTEN MOOD AND WITH A headache. There were no birds singing this morning. She hadn't seen Matt since the day after she'd come home from New York, the morning she woke with him in her bed. She couldn't believe he hadn't been by to bug her. Jessie asked her brothers, but they'd not seen him either. *Could Matt be giving in to her wish to call it quits? Maybe he was ready for a divorce. Damn!* But she wasn't certain that was what she wanted.

She didn't want to be just *Matt Whitaker's wife.* She needed to be her own person. She couldn't maintain her identity without divorcing him. And she certainly couldn't have an independent career while hidden away on the ranch. As much as she hated the idea, it seemed like divorce was the only answer.

She sat in her studio staring at the incomplete illustrations, unable to focus and knowing she must to make her deadline. Ideas wouldn't come, and, when they did, they wouldn't flow through her fingers to the drawing board.

Frustrated at not getting any work done, Jessie headed to the kitchen for a cup of coffee. While it was brewing, a knock came at the door. When she opened it, she was surprised to see her husband standing there. "Matt, why did you knock?" she asked. "Why didn't you just come in like you always do?"

"Because I doubt you like me walking in and making myself at home," he said.

"I guess I was kind of cranky the last time I saw you."

After he closed the door, Matt presented Jessie with a small bakery box.

"What's this?"

"I stopped by the general store. Millicent had fresh-baked scones. So I brought some for a midmorning snack—if you have time or can make time."

"Absolutely. I just brewed myself a cup of coffee. Come into the kitchen and I'll make you one—strong, hot, and black, right?"

Jessie removed her mug of vanilla biscotti from the Keurig and started a cup of morning blend for Matt. He got plates from the cupboard and put the scones onto the table in the breakfast nook.

"Matt, these are wonderful. Thank you for bringing them. I have been at sixes and sevens all morning, unable to make anything work. I needed this break."

"In that case, I'm glad I intruded," he said.

Jessie was trying to figure out what was different about Matt. He didn't seem like his usual in-your-face self. He seemed reserved, almost shy. *What was that all about?*

"Matt, is something wrong?" she asked. "You don't seem like yourself."

"No, nothing's wrong. I just came to ask if you have anything planned for Jordan's birthday next month."

"No, no plans. Why?"

"I've been itching to throw a big barbecue," Matt explained, "and the occasion of Jordan's birthday seems like a good excuse. What do you think?"

"A barbecue sounds like a good idea," Jessie said, then hesitated. "But I don't think Jordan will want a birthday party."

"I'll talk him into it. But I wanted to make certain you didn't already have plans. Weather should be good by then. Sometimes we have snow flurries in late spring, but that won't stop the folks around here."

"You should check with Kat to see if she has any plans," Jessie pointed out.

"Right, I still haven't gotten accustomed to the idea that Jordan has a wife."

"Neither have I," Jessie replied. "I never thought I'd see the day."

Matt stood. "Thanks for the coffee."

"Where are you going?" Jessie felt almost petulant.

"I don't want to interrupt your work since you have deadlines and stuff."

Jessie wasn't ready for Matt to leave. *What was happening?* Usually she had to throw him out the door, but today he seemed ready to go on his own.

"Come back to the studio and look at what I'm working on. You might give me some ideas. My creative well seems to have dried up."

Matt followed her into her studio. She

watched him look at the illustration board on her drafting table. She knew he loved her—therefore he loved all her work. Not that he lied about what he thought of her efforts; he just liked everything she did.

"These illustrations are for the Colorado Visitors Bureau in Denver," she said. "The plan is to use them in an advertising campaign next year, one designed to bring tourists to the state in the summer. I've hit a dead end—unable to find the right inspiration. I need something to pop off the page."

"How about this? *Come get high in Colorado!*"

Jessie thought about the slogan. Yes, she could work with that. She'd curve the slogan so the word *high* peaked at the top of the curve. She'd use mountains, and airplanes to show travel, and fluffy clouds to indicate floating above troubles. If the recreational use of pot was legalized in Colorado in the November elections, then the catch phrase would be a double entendre. And if she did other illustrations with skiers on those mountains, the state might use her illustrations to encourage winter tourism.

"Matt, you're a genius," she declared. She threw her arms around him and kissed him on the lips.

What started out as a kiss of gratitude quickly became a kiss of passion. He pulled her against his hard body. His arms tightened around her. She felt safe and loved. All the frustration of the morning dropped away. She also felt heat and desire. Her body wanted this man.

She pulled away, knowing if she didn't she would drag him into the bedroom. All her efforts to separate from him and his love would be undone. She didn't think she would be able to start over again. She loved him too much, but she needed to be true to herself. Otherwise, he'd smother her.

Matt looked stunned when she jerked out of his arms. It was as if she had slapped him. "What was that all about?" he asked.

"I'm sorry, Matt. We got carried away. It's not a good idea for us to go too far."

"Too far? Jessie, we're married—we can't go too far."

DRIVING THE ROAD FROM SPRUCE CREEK TO Grant, Matt thought of the cliché "all's fair in love and war." If that were true, he would wage a campaign against his wife's ambivalence—one he intended to win. He'd bring in the heavy artillery.

His first stop in Grant was at Largo Construction. Here in the high country a firm couldn't afford to be too specialized, so Largo did all kinds of construction. The boss man, Luis Largo, was in his office when Matt arrived.

"*Hola*, Matt. What can I do for you?"

Matt grinned at the big, burly man and embraced him in a man-hug. Matt genuinely liked Luis, and Luis genuinely liked the whole world. "I have two, maybe three, jobs for you. The first thing I want you to do is run a grader up and down my ranch road and all the ancillary roads around the ranch house. I want them scraped level, ruts filled and smoothed, and a bed of gravel spread over the surfaces."

"Wow, Matt, that's a big job. Going to be plenty expensive."

"I can afford it, Luis. Next, I want you to build a studio for Jessie out behind the house, two rooms with a half bath. The larger room should be all insulated glass, lots of light but warm enough for her to work during the winter. So the studio will need a good in-floor heating system. The other room she can use for an office, lots of outlets for computers and stuff. I need it completed in a month. Can you get drawings done right away?"

"A month? You're in a hurry. I'll drive up in the morning to look over where you want to build, discuss sizes and finishes. You're going all out, so I guess the rumor about you and Mrs. Whitaker breaking up isn't true?"

"Too many people in this county know too damn much about my personal life. With any luck, building her a studio will put an end to that rumor," Matt growled. "But I don't want Jess to get even a hint of this project. So you're sworn to secrecy and, once you start construction on the studio, your crew will need to keep their lips zipped."

Luis grinned, appearing delighted to be part of a conspiracy.

"As for the third potential project," Matt continued, "I'll know more when I see you tomorrow. I'm going to Denver to talk to a buddy of mine about installing a satellite link at the ranch. Then Jessie can have phone and Internet service for her business."

Luis walked Matt out to his Range Rover. "I'll have the grader at work tomorrow on the ranch road. The sooner it's graded and graveled, the sooner I can haul materials to the construction site. And I'll bring cost estimates and contracts tomorrow."

"Thanks, Luis. You're a good man. Come up in time for breakfast and I'll have Consuela prepare *huevos rancheros.*"

Matt was very pleased with himself as he drove down Highway 285 toward Denver. *I'm on a roll.* He was confident he'd have the road and studio completed by the time of Jordan's birthday party. The satellite link might be more problematic. But his buddy Chuck would have the answers he needed.

As Matt came down through the foothills and the elevation decreased, the temperature climbed. He opened his windows and enjoyed a warm spring breeze. Springtime in the Rockies was everything the lyricist claimed. He loved all the seasons in Colorado. He was rich enough he could live anywhere in the world, but he'd been nowhere he liked better than where he lived now.

As soon as he drove into Jefferson County, he hit heavy traffic. The suburbs were pushing farther west every day. He made his way across the sprawl of Lakewood and came to the Denver city limits. Chuck's company was in Larimer Square, at the west end of downtown, so Matt didn't need to drive all the way across Denver. He found parking at Twenty-first and Arapahoe, and then walked three blocks to his buddy's office.

In college, Chuck and he had been frat brothers and roommates. Matt worked on a business degree with an emphasis on agribusiness. Chuck absorbed all there was to learn about electronics, computers, communications, and all things technical. What Chuck didn't know, he could find out.

After they'd settled into Chuck's comfortable chairs, Matt explained he wanted to establish Internet communications from his mountain ranch.

"I think I need something with the sophistication of the system set up at McMurdo Station." Matt laughed at his grandiose description. "Something able to function in all temperatures and weather. I want to bounce signals off communications satellites circling overhead and send those signals around the world."

Chuck had visited the ranch a few times, so he had an idea of the challenges involved. "Wow, Matt, no half-way measures for you."

He agreed to drive up to the ranch the following morning to look over the terrain and meet with Matt's contractor. And while it was unlikely he would come in contact with Jessie,

Chuck also swore to keep the project secret.

Satisfied with his accomplishments so far, Matt decided on one more stop. There was a jewelry shop nearby that had excellent Native American pieces. Precious gems didn't impress Jessie, but she loved fine silver and turquoise, agate, and opal. Matt went shopping for a peace offering Jessie wouldn't be able to resist. He found a hand strung liquid silver and green turquoise Concho necklace he knew she would love. And because he wanted to go over the top, he bought a matching bracelet and earrings. He was hoping for another kiss of gratitude that turned into passion.

Torrey had told him he had to court her. He was launching a campaign to win her back, and now he prepared to lob the first salvo of the battle. Jessie would never know what hit her.

THREE

Jessie breezed through the back door of the clinic determined to see her brother. "Morning, Torrey," she greeted the office manager. "Is Jordan in his office?

"Yes, but . . ."

Jessie nodded and pressed on. She pushed her brother's door open, and almost backed out when she saw her husband seated in the visitor's chair in front of Jordan's desk.

"Abe's bitch is about to whelp," her brother was saying. "You might be able to buy one of the pups to train as a herd dog. Of course, since the sire was a midnight traveler, you can't be certain exactly what you'll get."

From the confused look on Matt's face, Jessie knew the two men hadn't been talking about dogs before she barged into the office. But she decided to let it pass. She could learn later the real topic of their conversation.

"Jess, you still haven't learned to knock before coming into my office," Jordan said, looking mildly irritated with his sister.

"And I doubt I ever will."

"Hi, Matt," Jessie said, turning to look at her husband. "What are you doing here?"

"I'm here talking to the local vet about animal stuff. What about you? Why are you here?"

"I came to ask my brother to take me to lunch."

"Sorry, Jess, I've eaten already," Jordan said, jumping into the conversation before it became contentious. "Kat had lunch on the table at precisely noon. But I'm sure your husband will be happy to take you to lunch."

"Oh." Jessie felt deflated. She'd wanted to talk with Jordan, to ask his opinion about her future with Matt. While younger than she, he was the head of the family now. Of course, she suspected how he would respond if she suggested divorcing Matt. As far as Jordan was concerned, Matt *was* family.

"It would be my great pleasure to take you

to lunch," Matt said, standing. "If you'd like, we can go to Pine Cone Café in Grant."

Jessie was uncertain if this was a good idea. Being with Matt left her feeling stirred up. Her girlie parts didn't always agree with her determination for physical restraint.

"Come on, Jess, it's only lunch. It's not like I'm suggesting a weekend at a hideaway in Aspen."

Jessie felt heat in her face and knew she was blushing. "Matt, must you embarrass me in front of my brother?"

"It's okay, Jess. Now that Jordan's married, he knows what loving couples do."

Jordan stood and moved toward the door. "Children, you may use my office for your private discussion. But I don't want to hear any yelling or screaming—it disturbs the customers. Close the door when you leave."

Matt grabbed his wife's hand. "We're right behind you, Bro," he said in a determined voice, while dragging Jessie along.

Jessie knew better than pitch a fit in the clinic. So she allowed herself to be led out of the office to Matt's Range Rover.

"We should take my Rover," Jessie said looking at the mud-splattered exterior of Matt's vehicle. "Mine is cleaner than yours."

"Mine is clean on the inside. Besides, I have something in here for you."

"What?" Jessie asked, surrendering and climbing into the passenger seat.

"You'll see," Matt responded. "Meanwhile, fasten your seatbelt."

Jessie nervously rubbed her palms on the tops of her thighs. The roomy interior of the Range Rover suddenly felt close and intimate. She knew she was a captive audience. Matt could talk about anything he wanted, and she had to stay and listen. She kept her eyes fixed on the window and the sights beyond.

Mercifully, he talked about general subjects and did not delve into any touchy topics. When they drove into Grant, Matt asked if she wanted to eat there or drive on into the town of Pine.

"Let's eat here," she answered. "I'd like to pick up some groceries before we go back to Spruce Creek. I'm running low on K-cups, and Millicent doesn't stock them in the general store. And if she did, I wouldn't be able to afford them."

"Jess, if you need money all you have to do is ask."

"I know that. I don't need money. It's only

that Millicent aims for one hundred percent profit on everything she sells."

Jessie preceded Matt into the restaurant. The majority of the lunch crowd had come and gone, so the waitress motioned for them to sit anywhere. They took a table by a window overlooking a patch of wildflowers.

"I'm so glad spring is on its way. Winter is really ugly in New York."

"How so?" Matt asked.

"Snow banks are black with soot and exhaust. And instead of the still peace we have here after a snowfall, in New York it's horns honking and voices yelling. That city is a cacophony of noise, even worse than Denver."

Jessie reached her hand across the table and tentatively touched her fingers to Matt's. "I want to thank you again for making my house ready for me. This last week I just fused myself, body and spirit, with my little abode. With no concerns about restoring the house to habitability, I've enjoyed being at home, sleeping in my own bed, cooking in my own kitchen, watching a fire in my own fireplace. Thank you."

Matt turned his palm up, slipped his fingers beneath Jessie's, and gently squeezed her hand. "That's all I wanted, to provide a safe haven for you—to offer you warmth and comfort—to let you know I care."

Jessie tensed and pulled her hand back. *Why couldn't the man accept a simple offer of gratitude without using it as an excuse for advancing his agenda?*

She was conflicted. She loved Matt, but she didn't know if she loved him enough to accept the lifestyle he wanted. She needed her career for her self-image, and that wasn't possible if she lived at the ranch. It was difficult enough living in Spruce Creek, but at least she wasn't trapped for months at a time. She had telephone and Internet access most of the time. She could get down to Denver if need be. She could . . .

MATT WAS RELIEVED WHEN THE WAITRESS arrived to take their order. Jessie appeared deep in thought. Matt watched as the intrusion snapped her back into the present.

Matt decided now was the time to start the courtship. "I was in Larimer Square yesterday on business. I stopped in a store that carries Native American jewelry. I got you something." He handed her the box with the Concho necklace.

He watched her open the gift. Her facial

expression turned from one of curiosity to one of wonder.

"Oh Matt, this is beautiful . . . green turquoise. But what's the occasion?"

"No occasion. Can't a man buy his wife a gift?" Matt was pleased Jessie was excited about the necklace. "There's more," he said handing her the second box with the earrings.

As she opened the second box, Matt watched her eyes change from wide surprise and pleasure to suspicion and doubt.

"Matt, this is over the top—what have you done?"

Matt was a patient man, but this was too much. "Damn it, Jess. Why must I be guilty of something? I saw this jewelry. I thought you'd like it. I bought it. I'm not guilty of anything except loving you."

"You can't blame me for being suspicious. In all the years we've been together, both before we were married and since, you've never given me anything like this."

"Well, I should have," he declared.

Matt knew their voices were rising. The patrons in the restaurant were looking their way. They needed to tone down their argument.

He reached for her hand again. "I missed you

while you were gone," he said quietly. "I realized I've taken you for granted, and I decided I would behave differently in the future."

The doubt and suspicion left Jessie's eyes. "I'm sorry," she whispered. "I always jump to conclusions."

He nodded. "I know. You always have, but it's part of who you are, and I love who you are. I have since the day we met, and I always will. But I'd be grateful if you stopped provoking me."

This time Jessie squeezed Matt's hand before withdrawing hers. Matt thought maybe he had made progress slowly, but moving in the right direction. He knew he now needed to back off a little and give her some room. Jessie did not respond well to being herded. Whenever that happened, she dug in her heels and became an immovable object.

When the waitress arrived with their meals, they were chatting companionably. They ate quietly, comfortable in each other's presence. They were discussing the advisability of dessert when Luis Largo walked in.

"*Hola,* Matt, Mrs. Whitaker, nice to see you both."

In his mind, Matt knew that Luis was ending the sentence with the word *together.* "Good to see you, Luis. Want to sit down and have dessert with us?"

"No, I'll pass. But, Matt, can you stop by the office before you leave town?"

"Sure. I'm going to drop Jessie off at the grocery to shop. I'll come by while she's stocking up."

"What was that all about?" Jessie asked.

"Don't know, but I'm certain I'll find out when I go by his office."

They decided against dessert and left the restaurant. Grant was a small town—not as small as Spruce Creek—but small enough. The drive to the grocery store took less than five minutes. Matt dropped Jessie and assured her he would be back in a half hour.

When he got to Largo Construction, Luis was ready for him. "I know you don't have much time, but I wanted to give you these sketches and notes along with a formal estimate for building Mrs. Whitaker's studio. I also included a covered walk from the house to the studio with a heated pathway. Then she will be able to go from house to studio in the winter with protection from the weather."

"Good idea, Luis. Thanks. If you come up with any other good ideas, let me know."

"You should give some thought to solar power up on your mountain top—expensive to install, but cheaper in the long run than propane generators."

"I'll think about it. But we need to get these three projects done first. Chuck was going to drive up to the ranch today to look at the challenge of setting up the satellite link. I'll have him stop here on his way back to Denver and discuss what he may need in the way of infrastructure. It will be soon. He knows the importance of speed."

The two men shook hands and Matt started to leave. He stopped and turned to Luis. "By the way, I'm hosting a big barbecue at the ranch on May nineteenth to celebrate Jordan Walker's birthday. I hope you'll come and bring the whole family."

"I'll check with Maria, but I'm sure we'll be there. Is this a surprise for Jordan?"

"No, I couldn't be certain the guest of honor would appear if he hadn't been persuaded in advance. So he knows. But he doesn't want any gifts, just the pleasure of your company."

"Thanks, Matt, I'm looking forward to it."

Matt pulled into a parking place as Jessie came out of the grocery store. He hurried to help her load the groceries into the back.

"Did you get everything you wanted?" he asked.

"Not exactly, but I did get everything I needed."

"There's a difference?"

"Of course," she responded. "I might want fresh asparagus, but I don't need it. I needed K-cups and I got them."

"Well, it is a good thing you didn't need fresh asparagus, because you aren't going to find it here in April." Matt laughed at her.

"I know, silly. I'm just arguing semantics with you."

"Let's go. I'll swing by the clinic so you can pick up your car and meet you at your house with the groceries," Matt said, while helping her into the passenger seat.

WHILE MATT UNLOADED THE GROCERIES AND carried them into the kitchen, Jessie opened the jewelry boxes and looked at the pieces again. They took her breath away, and she felt badly for being so suspicious of Matt's motives. She carried them into her bedroom and locked them in a drawer. There was virtually no crime in Spruce Creek, except for that burglary incident last year involving her sister-in-law, but better safe than sorry.

When she returned to the kitchen, Matt had carried in the last of the groceries and begun putting them away. "Matt, stop. I can do that."

"Who do you think put them away before you came home from New York?"

"I know you did, but that's not the point. It's my kitchen and I can put my own groceries away." Jessie couldn't figure out why she was being so sharp with Matt. *What's wrong with me?*

In a less confrontational voice, she asked Matt to stay for coffee. He accepted her invitation, and while she put items in the cupboard he started to brew her vanilla biscotti. She set out a plate of coconut macaroons she'd purchased at the store. After her coffee finished brewing, Matt started a mug for himself. They settled into the breakfast nook for the dessert they had denied themselves while in Grant.

"Matt, you need to see the work I've done on the *Come get high in Colorado!* campaign. I can't thank you enough for that slogan. I sent some sample ideas to the visitors bureau and they love the concept. I credited you for the slogan, so they'll send you a contract and a check."

"That's not necessary. I meant for you to get credit."

"It *is* necessary. They need to protect themselves from any possible claim of intellectual property theft. So you'll be asked to sign a contract giving the Colorado Convention and Visitors Bureau ownership of the slogan, and you'll be paid for your idea."

"You know I don't need the money. What's that cliché? Carrying coals to Newcastle? I'm the last person they should be giving money to."

"Then donate it to some worthy cause. But you must accept it or they won't use the slogan, and I won't sell my illustrations."

"Okay, I don't want to mess up your business opportunity. I'll sign the contract and I'll cash the check. I can use the money to buy you fresh asparagus."

Jessie felt warm inside. Matt really was a nice guy, even when he was exhibiting his boss-man attitude. And he was a great lover. If only he didn't live beyond civilization. The drive on the ranch road was barely endurable. The hum of generators went on for twenty-four hours every day. You had to drive to the highest elevation on the ranch to get even poor iPhone reception. The ranch was virtually cut off from outside contact. And that was only *one* of the problems with their marriage. There were others, even more contentious. Matt wanted children and she didn't. How does one overcome that obstacle? One can't, Jessie told herself.

Jessie led Matt into her studio. She had a half dozen illustration boards propped about the room, all variations on the *Come get high in Colorado!* concept. She was proud of her illustrations and hoped Matt would compliment her work. Sometimes she thought he didn't take her work seriously, that he thought it was some sort of a hobby. That was one of the reasons she was so insistent on living alone in her own little house. Why she had traveled to New York to study and to meet with publishers who would connect her with children's authors looking for illustrators. And one reason why she would probably divorce him. Her heart ached at the thought.

"Jessie, these are wonderful," Matt said. "If I didn't already live in Colorado, I certainly would be persuaded to vacation here. No wonder the visitors bureau is impressed. How will they use the illustrations?"

"They'll be used next year as ads in

magazines, on TV, and on the Internet. They'll appear in vacation brochures distributed at travel conventions and sent to travel agencies all over the world. Large wall-sized illustrations will be used at airports to encourage business travelers changing planes at places like DIA and Colorado Springs to return with their families on vacation. I'm so excited."

"How do you get paid? Do you get a one-time flat fee payment, or do you get some type of royalties?"

"I have a contract for a certain number of impressions, tens of thousands, which will pay me a generous lump sum. But if they exceed that number or place the ads in additional venues, like out-of-state airports, then I'll receive additional royalties."

"How did you get this commission?" Matt asked.

"The state sent out an IFB last October."

"What's an IFB?" Matt asked.

"It's an Invitation for Bids. I submitted and I was awarded the contract in January, contingent upon acceptable campaign illustrations delivered by the end of May. Thanks to you, I was able to meet the deadline."

"What would have happened if you hadn't

made the deadline?"

"They would have gone with some in-house designs like they do most years. They've already committed for ad space in the May, June, and July issues of all the major travel magazines next year. The agency will send the ad copy electronically, and the campaign will be underway."

"Did you have an attorney look at the contract?"

"Yes, I engaged an intellectual property attorney in New York. He reviewed the contract before I signed it. He ensured everything is in order. I wouldn't expect any kind of funny stuff dealing with the State of Colorado, but my interests are protected just in case."

"I'm proud of you, Jess. You really are in business for yourself. You're now a professional illustrator."

Jessie suspected Matt was just patronizing her. She didn't believe he took her seriously—at least, he never had before. *Why should he start now?*

FOUR

Early in May, ten days before the planned birthday barbecue, Matt stood on the front porch of the ranch house and waited anxiously for Jordan and Kat to exit their SUV. He grinned as Jordan lifted Kat out of the vehicle. He remembered how Kat used to rebuke her husband for treating her like a pet. But it was a fact—she had been too petite to get in and out of the SUV on her own.

"What do you think of the road?" Matt asked. "Is it improved enough that Jess will feel comfortable driving on it?"

"I think it's great," Kat said. "I didn't bite my tongue once. You got rid of all the potholes."

"Luis and his crew did a great job," Jordan added. "Nicely crowned and deep ditches at the sides. You'll need to maintain it, of course. But it really beats driving on a rutted dirt track and bogging down in the mud."

"Well, it won't get a lot of traffic, so maintenance shouldn't be too difficult. But I realize if I don't keep it up, Jess won't consider it easy access, so it will be maintained."

Matt watched Jordan look at some of the other obvious improvements. He knew his brother-in-law's opinion would foretell how Jessie would react.

"Jordan, what do you hear?" Matt asked earnestly.

"Nothing—it is absolutely quiet. Wow! I don't hear the hum of the generators." Jordan sounded impressed.

"They're gone, in storage, and kept only for emergencies." Matt grinned. "I've replaced them with solar power."

Matt watched with pride as Kat and Jordan walked around the ranch house. When they got to the back and saw Jessie's studio, they both stopped and stared.

"Can we look inside?" Kat asked.

"Sure, the studio's not quite done yet. It needs interior paint and finished flooring, but you can anticipate the completed project."

Matt showed them the covered walkway between the ranch house and the studio. He proudly pointed out the solar panels on the sloped roof and a tall steel antenna on a concrete pad at the end of the studio building.

He could tell Kat was impressed with all the glass in Jessie's studio. The wall that backed up to the half-bath was covered with drawers and shelves to be used for materials storage. The overhead lights could be individually controlled to cast light and shadow in whatever direction Jessie might desire.

Matt led them into the area set aside for Jessie's office. There were a few outlets in the floor, but most were set at waist level and at intervals of every four feet. He proudly pointed out a satellite phone and Internet connection waiting to be used. He bragged that Jessie would be able to reach anywhere in the world from her mountain-top retreat.

"What do you think?" Matt asked. "Can your sister be happy here now?" He held his breath while he awaited Jordan's reply.

Jordan looked around and nodded before answering. "You appear to have resolved every objection Jessie had to living on the ranch. I certainly hope she appreciates the effort you've exerted. She should be willing to be reconciled now. If she isn't, I've no idea what else she might want."

Matt didn't reply. He knew what else Jessie wanted, but that was between him and his wife—he wouldn't be discussing that subject with his brother-in-law.

"What can we do to support your efforts?" Kat asked after a few moments of silence.

"There *is* something—you and Jordan can help by keeping silent about all of the changes. I don't want Jess to suspect anything until she sees everything on the day of the barbecue."

Kat looked toward her husband. "Okay, we can do that, can't we, Jordan?"

"Also," Matt continued, "ask Jess to drive up with you on the day of the party. I want her to stay here for a few days. There may be other overnight guests, people who can't be expected to drive home to Denver or farther. But if she doesn't accept my invitation, I want you to be called away unexpectedly, abandoning her here. Can you do that?"

This time it was Jordan who looked at Kat. "We can do that. But my sister will commit mayhem on my body if she decides we plotted against her."

Changing the subject Matt asked, "Are there any people you would particularly like me to invite? Jess will be sending out the last-minute invitations tomorrow or the next day."

"I would like to see some of my frat brothers," Jordan said. "I can give Kat the names and email addresses. I'm assuming you've already invited everyone in Park County."

"Just about. You know what happens—you invite ten people and tell them to spread the word that everyone's welcome. They each tell ten more people and, before you know it, anyone who's ever heard your name is invited."

"You've told everyone there are to be no gifts," Jordan stated emphatically.

"Pretty much. Most people don't even know it's a birthday party. They just think I'm throwing a big barbecue," Matt said. "The only reason we used your birthday as an excuse is because that's the only way I could be sure Jess would come to the ranch. This really is an elaborate plot to get my wife to come back to me."

"You love her a lot, don't you Matt?" Kat asked.

"I love her more than life itself—even when she provokes me—and I'll do whatever it takes to win her back."

"It seems to me," Kat said, "that Jess will recognize that when she becomes aware of the efforts you've made.

LATE THE NEXT MORNING JESSIE, HEARING A knock, opened the front door to find her new sister-in-law on the porch. "Hi, Kat, come in." She welcomed Jordan's wife to the cozy warmth of her home, dragging her in out of a drizzly overcast.

"Jess, is this a good time? I don't want to interrupt if you are working."

"Now is a good time. I'm just taking a coffee break. Will you join me?"

"Thank you, yes. I'd love a cup."

Jessie ushered Kat into the kitchen and started the Keurig. "You're always welcome here you know, and there's no need for you to knock. Just come in and call out. That's what my brothers do. Now you're family too."

Kat's gamin grin lit up her face. "I've always wanted a sister, and now I have one."

"Me too," Jessie said, giving Kat a hug.

The two women settled into the breakfast nook and chatted like old friends. Kat explained the reason she stopped by was to bring Jessie the names and email addresses of additional invitees to the birthday barbecue.

They decided to get the invitations taken care of immediately. So Jessie led Kat back to her little studio. Kat looked around with obvious appreciation. "Jordan told me you're doing the illustrations for a Colorado tourism campaign. These look wonderful."

"Go ahead and browse." Pointing to her left, Jessie said, "Against that wall, I have some illustrations for a children's book."

Jessie made quick work of sending the invitations. Then she gave her attention back to Kat. "Most of my work is stored electronically. I just don't have room to keep the original drawings here."

"I can see that. Your studio is kind of cramped."

"You make do with what you have," Jessie replied. "After a year in New York, I know I don't want to live anywhere else but here in the Colorado High Country, so I traded a large design space in the studio the study group used in exchange for clean air and peaceful surroundings."

For just an instant Jessie thought Kat had the

strangest look on her face. Then, whatever the cause, it disappeared. "Kat, if you're not needed back at the clinic right away, stay for lunch. My brother can fend for himself."

"Okay, but let me call him so he knows I'm not coming back immediately."

Jessie eavesdropped on the phone call without compunction. She wanted to know how this petite, freckle-faced redhead had captured the heart of her misogamist brother. She was disappointed, however, when the conversation was no different than what any assistant might have with the boss when failing to return to work as expected.

Kat settled at the table, and Jessie served homemade vegetable soup and BLTs. "Jess, this is just right for a cold day. I hope conditions are better for Jordan's barbecue."

"Oh, I'm certain they will be. You know what they say here in Colorado, if you don't like the weather, just wait five minutes."

Jessie sat across from Kat. "So, tell me—I'm dying to know how you roped my brother into marriage." Jessie blushed. "Oh, that sounds insulting, as if you set out to take advantage of him, and I'm certain you didn't. No one has ever made Jordan do anything he didn't want to do. I just never expected him to marry."

A dreamy look swept over Kat's face. "It was just the opposite—Jordan swept me in and held me hostage until I agreed to marry him."

Jessie listened to Kat tell the story of how she came to live in his apartment. Of how Jordan had acted with propriety until he suspected—incorrectly—that Jeremy might have an interest in Kat. And how finally he had wooed her and, after much turmoil, decided he wanted them to marry. Kat didn't share the trauma that almost destroyed their happy ending.

"Jordan's not big on moonlight and flowers, but I have no doubt he loves me. He's my shelter in a storm and my rock in quicksand."

"Of course he loves you. He would never have married if he didn't," Jessie said. "But I must know—am I going to be an aunt? Is that a baby bump I see? You are such a little thing. It can't be anything else."

Kat's smile grew as she shared her excitement at her impending motherhood. "Yes, I'm six months along, and even wearing loose tops, I've begun to show. You're going to be an aunt at the end of August. Jordan and I are both ecstatic."

"That's something else I never expected— Jordan becoming a father. I don't know how much you know about our childhood, but Jordan still bears the scars of being abandoned by our mother when he was six. He finds it hard to trust, and I've never seen him risk love before. I'm so happy for you both."

"Turn-about is fair play," Kat said. "Tell me about your marriage. It is obvious Matt loves you more than anything, and I think you love him. But still you live apart."

"Our marriage is very complicated. We've loved each other since high school. He saw me through some difficult times raising Jeremy. He waited patiently until Jeremy was grown and I felt free to marry. During that time, Matt was never demanding or controlling." Jessie took a deep breath, "Now that I am establishing a career, however, he seems to want to deny me my independence. He wants me to live at the ranch and I can't."

"Why can't you?" Kat asked.

"You've been there. It's remote. It's in a cone of communication silence. There's no iPhone reception. I can't run a business when I can't interact with clients. And there are other reasons."

"Other reasons you don't want to talk about?"

"That's right," Jessie responded.

"But it's obvious you love him. When the two of you are in the same room, sparks fly. Your emotions are on the edge of spontaneous combustion. I expect Matt to drag you off to a bedroom at any moment."

"Oh, there is lust and passion, but I don't think that is enough for a marriage to endure. We want different things, Matt and I. We have what I call irreconcilable differences."

"Well, in my opinion, you should give into the lust and passion. It will either burn itself out or resolve those differences."

"I'm afraid to. I'm afraid I'll be consumed—that I'll lose my sense of *self*. I'm afraid Jessica Walker Whitaker will cease to exist leaving only Matt Whitaker's wife. This struggle is hard because I do love him so much. But it's taken me more than a year to get where I am today, and I'm not going to surrender the ground I've gained."

LATE THAT AFTERNOON, LONG AFTER KAT HAD gone back to the clinic, Jessie sat in her studio and stared at the four walls. She liked her little studio, but as Kat had pointed out, it was cramped. Maybe she could move some of the stuff that wasn't used frequently to the dining room. She rarely had dinner guests. Close friends and family could eat in the kitchen as they always did when visiting.

Walking into the dining room and looking around, she decided to box up her china and set it aside in a corner. She wouldn't get rid of her good dishes. They were wedding gifts and, even though her marriage was rocky, she couldn't bear to part with them. When that was done, the china hutch would be available to store illustration boards and drawer space would be free for inks, pens, paints, and brushes.

As she was moving china from the hutch to the dining room table to begin wrapping and boxing, she heard the kitchen door open and close. She wasn't worried. As she'd told Kat, family just walked in and called out. She was surprised, however, to hear the sound of her husband's voice. She couldn't imagine what Matt was doing down in Spruce Creek so late in the day. Unless he planned on staying the night, he should be well on his way to the ranch by now.

"Hi, Jess, where are you?"

"I'm here in the dining room."

He walked into the room and looked at her with curiosity. "What're you doing, honey?"

"I'm boxing up the china and silver. I'm outgrowing my studio so I'm going to move some of my supplies in here."

"What will you do if you want to have company?"

"I'll cross that bridge when I get to it. What are you doing in town so late?"

"I came to have dinner with my best girl."

"Are you seeing someone?" Jessie asked in a breathless voice. She'd been afraid Matt was going to get tired of her standoffish behavior, but she wasn't prepared for it to happen so soon.

"Yes, you goose, I'm seeing you."

He pulled a bouquet of flowers from behind his back. "These are for you," he said, pushing the flowers in her direction. "And I have wonderful lamb chops in the kitchen awaiting my masterful touch on the grill."

Jessie couldn't remember Matt ever bringing her flowers. They hadn't had that kind of relationship leading up to their marriage. When they'd had dinner together, she'd always cooked because she'd needed to cook for her brothers and Matt just joined the family at the dinner table.

"I brought baking potatoes and all the

trimmings. I also brought a lovely bottle of Bordeaux. Put the china back in the hutch, sweetheart, and set the dining room table. We'll dine on fine dinnerware by candlelight."

"Matt, what are you doing?"

"I thought it was obvious," he said with a shrug. "I'm going to cook dinner for you."

"That's not what I mean. Why are you being so nice?"

"I'm courting you, wife." Matt leaned down and kissed her forehead. "It was pointed out to me recently that I take you for granted. We never had a normal courtship. We fell head over heels in love the day we met, and we married as soon as I graduated college and you were free of your child-rearing responsibilities. You went from being the surrogate mother of two boys to being an instant wife. You never had the opportunity to experience being wooed as a young woman."

"But I wanted to be your wife then. I'm just not certain I do now."

"That's why I'm courting you. I'm going to convince you that you do want to be my wife— now."

Matt disappeared into the kitchen and Jessie set the table using the fine china she had been preparing to stow away. *No problem—she could pack it tomorrow or the next day.* Meanwhile, it would be fun to have a dinner date with her somewhat estranged husband. She had no idea how to describe her relationship with Matt.

She placed a vase with the flowers in the center of the dining room table. She lit candles on both sides of the vase and dimmed the lights. She could do romantic. If he was courting her, then maybe he wouldn't expect her to fall into bed with him at the end of the evening. Proper couples didn't do that on a first date.

When she slipped into the kitchen to offer her help, Matt chased her off to the living room where he'd lit a fire. He handed her a glass of wine and instructed her to sit down and put her feet up.

When he led her into the dining room, he pulled out her chair, and, after she was seated, draped a napkin over her lap. "See, just like the fancy restaurants," he told her, "and you don't need to tip the waiter."

After she was pleasantly full on a perfectly charbroiled lamb chop with tossed salad, baked potato, and fresh asparagus—*where did he find fresh asparagus in Colorado in early May?*—he escorted her back to the parlor with instructions to stay put.

"You can't put the china in the dishwasher,"

she called after him.

"Don't worry. I'm washing the dishes by hand.

"Are you sure I can't help?" she asked. "I could dry the dishes."

"I really wanted to make tonight special for you, Jess. I don't want you feeling you have to be a housewife."

"What if I want to share domestic chores with you? We don't do much together anymore."

The wine was obviously making her feel mellow. *Why was she so anxious for her husband's company? Why not?* Matt was a fine looking man and a wonderful lover. Without further thought, she picked up the dish towel and started drying the china and silver. She placed each piece on the table. Tomorrow would be soon enough to put everything away.

FIVE

MATT ROLLED ONTO HIS BACK AND STRETCHED, suffering no disorientation waking in Jessie's bed. He knew exactly where he was and why. He had made love to his wife last night—all night—in a most satisfying manner. Hopefully, Jessie had enjoyed it as much as he had. Based upon her responses, he thought she had.

He embraced his wife's pillow and buried his nose in her scent. He wanted to wake to her essence every morning for the rest of his life.

Eventually, Matt got out of bed, pulled on his briefs and jeans, and followed the smell of brewing coffee into the kitchen. Jessie hummed as she moved about setting out napkins and flatware.

She wore a short sexy sleep shirt. He

stepped behind her and wrapped his arms around her. "Good morning, beautiful wife," he whispered in her ear as he pulled her butt firmly up against his erection.

"Good morning, you randy old goat," she retorted.

She smiled, and didn't pull away, so Matt knew all was well in his world this morning. "May I take my beautiful wife out to breakfast?"

"No way! If we go out together this early in the day people will know we slept together last night."

"Married people do that, you know. It's acceptable. In fact, it's encouraged."

"But last night was our first date. Proper couples don't sleep together on a first date."

"Last night was our second date, my sweet. Don't you remember? I took you to the senior prom."

"Oh, well, in that case I guess it's okay if we slept together." Jessie giggled. "But we still can't go out to breakfast because I baked pecan cinnamon rolls for you this morning."

"Jess, my sweet, you know those are my favorites. What's the occasion? Are you courting me now?"

She looked at him with a generous smile, a

smile that lit up her eyes and warmed his heart as well as other parts of his anatomy farther south. "I figured if you could get me fresh asparagus, I could bake your favorite breakfast treat," she said.

"Then you noticed the asparagus last night. I wasn't certain you had. You didn't say a word."

"I didn't want to give you a swelled head."

They kept up the friendly banter while they drank coffee and munched on the homemade delicacies.

They heard the door open. "Hey, Jessie, are you decent?" Jeremy called out.

"She's not," Matt answered, "but since you're family you may come in anyway."

Jessie squealed and dashed into the bedroom. She reappeared modestly clad in a full-length robe. "I don't want to scandalize my little brother," she said, entering the kitchen.

"I won't be scandalized if I may have a few of those pecan cinnamon rolls. Please?" Jeremy whined.

"Those are mine," Matt said. "Jess made them for me."

"In return for what?" Jeremy quipped. "As if I didn't know."

"None of your business," Jessie answered.

"It's not hard to figure out, since neither you

nor Matt is dressed. And if Matt doesn't share his treats, I'll spread it all over town that he spent the night."

"So what? We're married," Jessie responded.

"So, you guys are back together again?"

"Well, not entirely. But we're working on it," Matt interjected.

"The town gossips will have a field day. Even in Grant, a consuming interest exists in the on-again/off-again Whitaker romance—more so than in the results of a Rockies game."

"Matt, give Jeremy a cinnamon roll, please," Jessie said, giving in to her brother's blackmail.

"You know, little brother," she told him, "you should be nicer to me. Someday you'll want something you won't be able to get by extortion, such as my silence when you meet the girl of your dreams. I'll make certain you're sorry for all the grief you've given me."

Matt observed the good-natured bickering between brother and sister. He loved the way the Walker siblings picked at each other until someone outside their family attacked one of them, and then they bonded together in an unassailable unit. He had felt that bond with his brothers-in-law and knew he was blessed to be considered a member of such a close knit group.

No matter what happened between him and Jessie, he wouldn't surrender his band of brothers.

Jeremy was eating his second roll when Matt looked up and asked him why he'd come to Jessie's this morning.

"Oh, I'm just delivering a message from Jordan and Kat. They want Jess to ride up to the ranch with them next weekend for the barbecue."

"Why didn't one of them just call?" Jessie asked. "They didn't need to send a personal messenger."

"Those two are so wrapped up in each other they wouldn't be able to find their way across the road to the clinic if they weren't holding hands. The chore of calling you would have fallen to Torrey—and she has enough to do. So I offered to deliver the message in person."

"You know, Jeremy, I don't care what folks say—you're a good kid," Matt quipped.

Jeremy grimaced. "You damn me with faint praise."

"Educated, too," Jessie added.

"Enough. Stop. No more. I'm leaving before this conversation deteriorates into a slapstick routine."

Jessie grinned. "Don't let the door hit you in

the fanny on the way out."

Matt pulled Jessie into his arms. "Now that your brother's gone, I sense a nap coming on. Let's slip into the bedroom for a bit of rest. Neither of us got much sleep last night."

"Go. Lock all the doors. I don't want any more family dropping in unexpectedly."

Before Matt could start securing the entrances to the house, the door opened again and Jeremy called out, "Jordan will pick you up at ten o'clock Saturday morning."

LATER IN THE AFTERNOON AFTER MATT HAD departed, Jessie busied herself putting away the china and stemware from the previous night's dinner. She ran the vacuum, changed her bed linens, put clean towels in the bathroom, and started a load of laundry. She knew she was just marking time and burning energy.

After last night and this morning, Matt undoubtedly believed all their problems were solved, and they were a couple again. But, troubled as she was, she knew they had settled nothing. All the same problems still existed.

Making a snap judgment, she resolved she'd

not go up to the ranch for the barbecue on Saturday. If she stayed away from Matt, he couldn't charm her back into his bed again. She knew her own weakness and if he were near, she'd not refuse him for long. After all, look what had happened during the last twenty-four hours. She'd behaved like a giddy young bride on her honeymoon.

Decision made, she marched into her bedroom and packed a small suitcase with enough items to last her a few days. She'd go to Denver and enjoy a mini vacation. The months of May and June in Denver were a pleasant time of year. Flowers would be in bloom and the temperatures warm enough the inversion layer would be gone. She'd visit museums, walk along Cherry Creek, and spend time hanging out at the Tattered Cover—her favorite book store.

She considered just leaving and not telling anyone where she went. But she couldn't do that. Her brothers would flip out and assume the worst—that she'd been kidnapped by space aliens or something equally ridiculous. So, as she tossed her suitcase into her Rover, she accepted she should stop by the clinic and leave word for Jordan.

In the late afternoon, she locked the door

behind her and slipped into her SUV. *Damn! She needed gas.* Well, she could stop in Grant before she hit the highway.

Entering the clinic through the back door, she went looking for Torrey. When she found her, Jessie immediately launched into her planned monologue. "Hi, Torrey," she said, giving her foster mother a hug. "I need you to give Jordan a message for me. Tell him I won't be going with him and Kat to the ranch next week. I need to go to Denver and I won't be back in time."

She muttered something about needing gas, almost ran from the clinic and, in her rush to get away, spun her wheels in the gravel lot. She slowed—the only thing speeding would do was raise dust and invite a deputy to delay her escape.

Her emotions were under control as she pulled into Hank's Fueling Stop and Snacks in Grant. The gas station sat on the right side of Highway 285, convenient for tourists heading southwest toward Kenosha Pass.

She chatted with Hank as he filled her gas tank. "Should I check the oil, Miss Jessica?" he asked her while he washed her windshield.

"No, thanks, Hank. I'm certain it's fine."

"One of your tires is a bit low. You might have a slow leak. I'll just add air for you. Don't want a flat, do you?"

"Thanks, Hank." Jessie steeled herself to tolerate these irritating delays. *Hank is right, I don't want a flat.*

When the gas tank was filled, the windows washed, and the tire inflated, Jessie began her getaway. Turning left across the highway, she headed east. There was no reason to rush, so she drove the posted speed limit. Yes, she was escaping, but no one would pursue her. Jordan would be disappointed, but he wouldn't come after her. Only Matt would do that, and since no one would be able to reach him, he'd not know she'd left Spruce Creek until it was far too late to do anything about her retreat.

Traffic was light. An occasional over-the-road trucker passed her from time to time, but they were the only vehicles she saw. Most people were home enjoying dinner with their families. No one drove this stretch of highway at this hour. Jessie relaxed and enjoyed the peaceful setting. She slipped a CD into the player and listened to blues music. Possibly not the best choice of entertainment, she realized—the smoky sounds would probably depress her.

As dusk descended, light and dark played across the road. Evergreens stirred in the breeze.

She'd made the right decision. Like the trees, she was too easily moved by the winds of her emotions. Maybe circumstances would force her to move to Denver. Spruce Creek lay much too close to the ranch. She needed more distance between Matt and herself.

Her mind wandered as she came around a curve and saw a large buck in the middle of the road frozen in her headlights. With no time to take evasive action, she stood on her brakes and then heard the thump of impact. The deer was thrown up on her hood, and her windshield shattered into a spider web of laminated glass. When the airbag deployed, she was saved from serious injury, but her vehicle would never be the same.

Grateful her phone showed three bars, she calmed herself and dialed 9-1-1. She told the dispatcher her location and what had happened. When she was asked to stay on the line, she explained she needed to get flares out around the bend in the road behind her. At the dispatcher's request, she agreed to leave the connection open so the State Patrol could track her on her phone's GPS.

Shaken by the experience, she still managed to get a large flashlight out of the back of her vehicle. She walked on the shoulder around the curve and placed flares as far in advance of the accident as possible. She was grateful she'd not been speeding. Of course, it would have been even better if she'd been more alert, but then she still might have hit the animal. Some things were fated.

MATT HEARD THE PHONE RING IN HIS OFFICE. No more than three or four people knew he had phone service at the ranch, and even fewer had the phone number.

"Whitaker," he answered.

"Matt, thank God I reached you," Torrey said, rushing her words. "It's Jess."

"Is she hurt? What's wrong?"

"No, she's not hurt. She's taken off for Denver. She stopped by the clinic on her way out of town. She left a message for Jordan that she wouldn't be going with them up to the ranch next week."

Damn! I must have spooked her.

"She said something about needing gas, so that'll slow her some if she stops to fill up."

"Thanks, Torrey. I owe you big time."

Matt hung up and yelled for his housekeeper. "Consuela. I'm going to be gone for a while. I probably won't be back tonight."

"But, *Señor*, you just got home."

"I know, but Jessie needs me."

He hastened out the door, into his Range Rover, and rushed down the ranch road at a speed that, even with the improvements, was excessive.

He hit Guanella Pass Road and continued south. The speed limit on the gravel portion of the road was twenty-five miles an hour. He was doing forty.

He cussed himself for rushing his reconciliation with his wife. She'd no knowledge about the changes at the ranch. She probably thought he was seducing her so she'd return and live with the restrictions that existed before. If he had been patient and waited until the barbecue, none of this would have happened.

He drove past the turnoff to Spruce Creek and slowed slightly. Not worried about getting a speeding ticket, he just couldn't afford to lose time by being stopped. So he came into the town of Grant at twenty-five miles an hour.

Pulling into the town's only gas station he called out, "Hey Hank, have you seen my wife?"

"She was here, filled up, and left about twenty minutes ago. She was headed east."

"Thanks," Matt called as he hit the gas pedal and was on his way northeast on Highway 285. He glanced at his own gas gauge and was relieved to see he had over three quarters of a tank.

His high beams cast light far ahead, so he focused and concentrated on the road. He was driving over the speed limit, but he didn't think his speed was unsafe. He was in control—of the vehicle, at least. Not in control of his emotions, he wanted to throttle his wife—she could push his buttons and provoke him to the extreme.

What was Jess thinking? She obviously wasn't—just reacting. Well, he was going to do some reacting. When he caught up with her, he was taking her to the ranch and keeping her there—no matter how much she protested.

He had been on the road for a while when he heard a siren behind him and saw flashing lights in his rear view. He pulled to the side of the highway. At first he thought he was going to be nabbed for exceeding the speed limit, but the State Patrol vehicle sped right past him. Matt had a bad feeling. He increased his speed and did his best to keep the patrol car in sight.

He heard the siren whine down ahead of

him. Then he saw the flares and slowed until he was stopped by an officer waving him to the side.

"There's an accident up ahead, sir. You need to wait until we've assessed the situation and have the road cleared."

"Can you tell me, is the vehicle involved a Range Rover? Is the driver a tall, dark-haired woman—very beautiful?"

"Apparently, you know her," the state patrolman replied. "She hit a deer, but her air bag deployed. She's unhurt except for a few bumps and bruises."

Jumping from his vehicle, Matt ran down the highway and around the curve. He rushed to embrace Jessie while she talked with another patrolman. "Oh my God, are you all right?"

The officer to whom she was speaking stiffened until Jessie spoke up. "It's okay, he's my husband."

Matt was overwhelmed with a mixture of emotions—love for his wife, gratitude she appeared uninjured, furious anger she'd run away, and a sense of hopelessness, fearing they would never get it right. He held her close and kissed the top of her head. He didn't dare speak because he didn't know what he might say.

"Matt. Matt, I'm okay. I'm not hurt. But I

killed a deer out of season." She giggled. Shock was setting in.

"Sir, there's an ambulance coming up from Lakewood. We didn't see a need for an air evac, but the EMTs will want to take her into the hospital to have her checked out."

"Can I bring my car around and follow her?

"Are your keys in your vehicle?"

Matt nodded. He was unwilling to let go of his wife, and he hugged her close.

The patrolman at the accident site radioed the officer stationed at the beginning of the flare warnings. He instructed him to drive Matt's car along the shoulder to where they were waiting.

Matt was grateful he hadn't been forced to leave Jessie to retrieve his car.

When the ambulance arrived, Jessie was loaded aboard and they started the journey down to the hospital. She was examined in the ER at St. Anthony's South. When no signs of concussion were found, she was given a sedative and Matt was allowed to take her home.

And take her home he did—home to the ranch.

SIX

WHEN JESSIE AWOKE, SHE ACHED OVER ALL OF her body. Even her hair ached. For a moment she didn't remember the night before, and then it all came back to her. She'd left Spruce Creek intending to go to Denver. She'd hit a deer and totaled the Rover. Somehow, Matt had been there. She couldn't figure out how that could've happened. He'd been with her at the hospital and then he'd taken her home—except not to her house in Spruce Creek. She realized he'd brought her to the ranch.

She lay in his bed, in his bedroom, in his ranch house. With a groan, she realized she wouldn't be going anywhere until Matt felt completely satisfied she'd recovered. And he wouldn't be easily satisfied.

How did she get herself into these situations? The ranch was the very last place she wanted to be. That's why she had decided to go to Denver, to avoid coming up to the ranch for Jordan's birthday barbecue.

Her brothers—did they know about the accident? They would go all macho on her—insist on driving her everywhere, never letting her behind the wheel again. She sighed. It wasn't only Matt she would need to battle to retain her independence. All three men would gang up on her.

Gingerly, avoiding stretching as much as she could, Jessie got out of bed and crossed the room to the en-suite bathroom. She looked in the mirror, dismayed to see the bruises on her face from the air bag. Her seatbelt had also locked—as intended—and she had an ugly welt over her shoulder and across her chest.

When she returned, she opened the draperies in the bedroom and saw she'd slept late into the morning. She also discovered she was starving, not having eaten since a late lunch the previous day. She was about to go in search of food when she heard a knock at the bedroom door.

"*Señora*, are you awake?"

"Yes, come in, Consuela. I'm awake and will

be glad to see a friendly face."

Consuela backed through the door carrying a tray filled with savory foods. She set the breakfast down on an occasional table near the bedroom fireplace.

"Please, *Señora*, you must again lay down. *Señor* Matt will not be pleased you have risen from the bed."

"He would be even less pleased if I had an accident in the bed as if I were a toddler."

At Consuela's blush, Jessie apologized. "I'm sorry, I didn't mean to embarrass you."

To make the housekeeper happy, she climbed back into bed and allowed Consuela to serve her breakfast. She enjoyed the *huevos rancheros* with black beans and *chorizo* and warm flour tortillas. She noticed with pleasure the coffee she sipped was her favorite, vanilla biscotti. Matt must have bought it in anticipation of her coming for the barbecue.

As she rested on the pillows propped against the headboard and savored her coffee, she realized there was something different. Something wasn't right. It was quiet. The constant hum of the generators was missing. *How could that be?*

"Consuela, I can't hear the generators. Do

you know why that is?"

"*Señor* Matt, he has people come who do strange things on all the rooftops, and now we have electricity without noise. Isn't it wonderful?"

"How long ago, Consuela? How long ago did this happen?"

"Last month, *Señora.* Big trucks came up on the new road. They brought lumber and concrete and windows and there was lots of pounding. But when everything was finished, we have blessed silence. At first it seemed very strange, but now I like it."

"Do you know where *Señor* Matt is now?"

"He went down the mountain to learn about your car, *Señora.* Said he will be back this afternoon and for you to stay in bed. He does not want you to wander about the house."

Jessie smiled to herself as the housekeeper left the room. Consuela had known there was no danger of Matt walking into the room and finding her up and moving. But she used the threat to make Jessie eat breakfast in bed.

Then Jessie began to wonder about other things. *Why wouldn't Matt want her to wander about the house? What other secrets did he have besides the conversion to solar power? And why keep that a secret?*

Giving serious thought to doing exactly what

her husband didn't want her to do, Jessie realized she had no clothes here. She wore a nightgown obviously belonging to Consuela, because it was too short for her. Maybe that was why Matt told Consuela not to let her go wandering around the house. Sometimes the ranch hands had reason to come in, and he wouldn't want the men seeing his wife in the housekeeper's nightgown.

Something else to worry about—clothes. Surely Matt would retrieve all the personal items from inside her Rover. As long as he brought the suitcase she had packed to take to Denver, she would have adequate clothing for a few days.

She was giving herself a headache thinking of all the problems caused by her accident. Obviously, fate hadn't intended her to escape to Denver. Her karma was she would be here for Jordan's barbecue. *I might as well lie back and accept my destiny.*

She scrunched farther down into the bed. Now that her stomach was full, she felt heavy-eyed. A little nap would not be unwelcome. As she drifted off to sleep, she dreamed she heard a telephone.

THE RANCH HOUSE WAS QUIET WHEN MATT came through the door. He wasn't yet used to the absence of the generator hum. Following tantalizing scents, he went to the kitchen in search of Consuela to get an update on Jessie's condition and, more importantly, her temperament. His housekeeper assured him his wife had eaten a good meal and then drifted back to sleep. Consuela told him she had looked in on Jessie from time to time and she was resting comfortably.

Matt was just happy Jessie wasn't rampaging through the house demanding to be taken back to Spruce Creek. He grinned. That event would undoubtedly come before long. Before carrying Jessie's suitcase into their bedroom, he went to his office to drop off all the documents resulting from his trip to the impound lot.

He opened the door quietly and saw she was still asleep. He left her bag next to the empty chest of drawers that had been hers when she had lived at the ranch after their marriage. He hoped, after all the effort and money spent to make the ranch more civilized, Jessie would settle in and call the ranch home once again. If she'd do that, then every penny spent would be an investment that yielded an immeasurable return.

When he turned, he found her looking at him with her eyes wide. "Matt, how's the Rover?"

"Totaled. Scrap metal. I met the insurance adjuster at the impound yard. The company will settle without argument. The State Patrol report indicated the accident was unavoidable."

"I'm so sorry. I tried to stop, but the animal was just there, standing in the middle of the road when I came around the curve. I wasn't speeding. I really wasn't."

Matt sat on the bed and enfolded his wife in his arms. "Jess, the Rover doesn't matter. What matters is you weren't seriously hurt. I can always buy another SUV, but I can never love another woman as I love you."

Jessie started to cry. Matt hugged her closer and let her weep away her stress and fear and guilt. The doctor had warned Matt this moment would come, and all he should do is endure.

Matt hated a woman's tears, and he especially hated Jessie's tears. He felt helpless. He wanted to make everything better for her, and he knew he couldn't. So he just held her and rubbed circles on her back and whispered loving words in her ear.

When she had cried herself out, Matt suggested a warm bath in the Whirlpool. She acquiesced and started to get out of bed.

"Stay in bed. I remember how you like it." Grinning, he formally bent at the waist. "I will prepare Madame's bath."

He ran warm water into the tub, added bath salts, and turned on the jets. He swept back into the bedroom and picked her up in his arms.

Laughing, Jessie struggled. "Matt, put me down," she said. "I can walk into the bathroom."

"If you don't stop wiggling, I'll drop you. Then you will be down, probably on your butt, not your feet."

When they got to the tub, Matt set her on the edge and pulled the nightgown over her head. Her bruises were more obvious this afternoon than they had been last night when he had put her to bed. *Thank God they were only bruises.* She would heal. Had she been speeding, had the air bag not deployed, had the road been wet or icy, he didn't want to think of what might have happened.

He helped her step into the tub and settle comfortably. He rolled a towel into a neck-rest and lit a scented candle. "May I bring you something to sip while you lounge in the bath?"

"I don't suppose a glass of wine would be a good idea."

"Probably not."

"Then you can bring me a glass of sparkling water over ice. I can sip on that while I soak the aches and pains out of my body."

Matt brought her the water she had requested, and then he settled onto the side of the tub. "Do you want me to stay and talk, or do you want to be left alone?"

"Stay. I have so many questions to ask you about things I don't remember."

"Such as?"

"I remember the accident. I remember calling 9-1-1 and setting out the flares. Then, after the State Patrol arrived, everything becomes fuzzy."

"You went into shock. It's not uncommon. Adrenalin kept you functioning until someone else arrived to take control. Then your mind ceded responsibility and withdrew."

"But I remember you at the scene of the accident, or at least I think I do. Were you there?"

"Yes, I was ten minutes behind you by then, so the State Patrol arrived just before I did."

"Were you following me? How did you know I was on the road? I thought you returned to the ranch after you left the house."

"Torrey phoned me the minute you fled the clinic."

"Phoned you, what do you mean phoned you? There's no telephone here at the ranch."

"There is now. When you finish your bath, I'll take you around to see the improvements I've made. I planned to show them to you next Saturday, but I'll move the great unveiling to this afternoon."

"So I didn't dream the sound of the telephone?"

Matt could tell she was impatient for the grand tour so he decided to accommodate her. He washed her hair, and then he helped her stand while he used the handheld shower to rinse her hair and body.

Her naked body was beautiful in spite of all the black and blue patches. He would be very gentle making love with her tonight.

AFTER JESSIE DRIED HER HAIR, DRESSED IN clothes retrieved from her suitcase, and made up the bed, she was ready for the tour. "I already know about the solar," she told Matt. "When I realized I didn't hear the hum of the generators, I asked Consuela. It wasn't hard to guess all the strange things on the roof tops our housekeeper told me about were solar panels."

Matt smiled. "Going solar in place of using propane generators will save tens of thousands of dollars a year. The mountain meadows will be silent, as they should be. And I still have the generators as back-up in the event the sun doesn't shine for a month."

"That's not likely. The sun shines somewhere in Colorado at least three hundred days a year," Jessie pontificated, sounding like a tour guide.

"Come on, I'll show you some of the solar storage cells. They're basically very big batteries. Like the generators, they supply electric current."

They walked out of the house hand in hand, the picture of the happily married couple Matt hoped they could be.

Jessie admired the level graveled drive in front of the house. "Is this what Consuela meant by a new road? It's nice to walk without turning an ankle in a muddy hole. How far does this improvement go?"

"All the way to the highway. That's one of the reasons I was so close behind you. Instead of ten miles an hour, I drove forty coming out the ranch road. I wouldn't recommend that for every day driving, but I'm grateful the road surface was graded and graveled as well as, or even better than, Guanella Pass Road."

"Wow! You have spent a ton of money. Tell me about the phone service."

"I would rather show you than tell you. Let's look at the solar cells first, and then we'll look at our own personal phone company."

Matt led her away from the house so she could see the solar panels gracing the roof. Then they went into a newly constructed shed, the interior of which looked like the equipment rooms atop high-rises in Denver. Obviously, she would have no idea what she was looking at, but he thought she would think it was impressive all the same.

Walking out of the equipment shed, Matt asked, "Jess, do you trust me?"

"Of course I trust you. I don't always agree with you, but I do trust you. Why do you ask?"

"Because I want you to close your eyes and let me lead you for a few minutes."

Jessie closed her eyes and stood very, very still. Matt put his right arm behind her back and then he walked slowly toward the back of the house, guiding her steps. He stopped and told her to raise her foot up onto a different surface.

"Okay, you can open your eyes." Matt had positioned her so that, when she opened her eyes, she was looking directly at a tall, steel antenna on a concrete pad. "That's our personal phone company. Everything is wireless and bounces off the communications satellites far overhead. So we now have telephone, Internet and, Consuela's favorite, satellite TV. The ranch has joined twenty-first century civilization."

"What's that building next to the antenna?"

"That, my dear wife, is the *pièce de résistance.*"

Leading her by the hand now that her eyes were no longer closed, Matt brought her along the covered walkway and handed her a key.

"Go on, open the door," he urged.

They stepped into a small anteroom with three closed doors. One to the right, one to the left, and one directly ahead. Matt opened the door to the right and ushered her into a completely outfitted office. There was a large desk holding a new laptop computer. "Wireless Internet connection anywhere in line-of-sight with the antenna. So you can work here in your office, or in the house, or up on the hill top."

Unable to judge how Jessie was reacting, he hurried on. Pointing to the phone, he said, "You have your own line for business, but you can also access the house phone line. And you can answer your business phone from inside the house."

Turning, he guided Jessie across to the other door and opened it into her studio. "You have east, west, and northern exposure," he said, opening the drapes electrically and bathing the studio in light. "The forth wall is composed entirely of storage space for your supplies. But if it doesn't meet all your needs, whatever else you want can be installed." Matt watched as Jessie looked over the studio.

"Where does the third door lead?" she asked.

"Half-bath," Matt opened the door into a charming powder room. "Say something, Jess. Your silence is killing me."

"I'm speechless. I don't know what to say. Are you trying to manipulate me? To get me to come back to the ranch?"

"If it's manipulation for a man to provide everything he can think of for the happiness of the woman he loves, then yes, I'm guilty of manipulation. You're my wife. I love you, and I want you living here with me at the ranch." He took a deep breath before continuing. "Everything you objected to was legitimate. You couldn't live here and pursue your career. I have done everything I could think of to erase your objections of being cut off from the outside world."

"There is still one major obstacle to us getting back together. And all these changes don't eliminate that problem."

"Jessie, I love you so much I'm willing to leave the decision of children entirely to you. I just want you back in my life, back in our home, and back in our bed. I do hope this is enough, because I am not willing to get cut."

"I'll try Matt. I *will* try. I'd be a real shrew if, after all you've done, I refused to meet you halfway." Jessie moved into her husband's arms and lifted her face for his kiss. "I do love you. I just don't know if I can live with you."

SEVEN

Saturday morning dawned sunny and bright. "Oh, the weather is perfect," Jessie said with a laugh, talking to herself. She was so pleased. Since it was only mid-May, it was too early in the season for any amount of heat in the High Country. As long as the sun is shining, the barbecue would be a success.

Jessie was looking forward to welcoming her family and friends to Whitaker Ranch. At Matt's urging, she had emailed invitations to some of her professional contacts along the Front Range.

Once the cat was out of the bag—that the purpose of the gathering was not exclusively to celebrate Jordan's birthday, but also an opportunity to welcome Jessie home—the guest list could be expanded to include friends and associates of Jessie's, as well. They would celebrate Jordan's birthday, but they would also enjoy festivities with other guests as part of the welcome activities.

The last week had been blissful. Jessie slept wrapped in Matt's arms every night. They gazed into each other's eyes over breakfast. They acted like honeymooners when they were together. But each day she also spent hours in her studio and office, just to prove she could live at the ranch and pursue a career at the same time. She felt she was succeeding.

Matt had driven her down the mountain to Spruce Creek a few days earlier to pack and move her boards and paints. The new road really was marvelous.

"You know," Matt had told her, "leaving valuables in the vacant house is unwise. Let Jeremy pack the rest of your belongings and bring them up to the ranch." So now their china would be in the ranch house dining room along with the fine stemware she and Matt had received as wedding gifts.

Since there was inadequate space to park one hundred cars—or even fifty—near the ranch house, guests were asked to leave their vehicles on Guanella Pass Highway and carpool to the barbecue site. So every car or truck that arrived was filled to overflowing with guests. They spilled out of vehicles talking and laughing. New friendships were made and old ones reestablished.

Jessie greeted everyone with a huge smile. She especially went out of her way to make her professional associates feel welcome. They'd all been warned to wear old comfortable jeans because Whitaker Ranch was a working ranch and not for fancied-up dudes.

"Let me show you my working space," she said as she led those professionals to see her studio. And, of course, she had to tell them how Matt had gone to all this effort to give her the best of both worlds—rustic ranch life and the life of a professional illustrator in touch with her clients around the globe.

When Jordan and Kat arrived, she took them to see all the improvements, unaware they'd seen them before. When they entered her studio, Kat said, "Oh, that color must be the same yellow you painted your kitchen in Spruce Creek."

"It is," Jessie agreed. "Matt chose that yellow because he knew how much I liked it."

Jordan, refusing to be drawn into decorating talk, asked Jessie when Matt would be ready to take possession of one of Abe's pups.

"Oh, I never thought that was a real discussion. I thought you guys were really talking about something else when I walked in, and the mention of the pups was just a cover-up."

"You have a suspicious mind, Sis. What would Matt and I have to cover up?" he asked her as his brother-in-law joined them.

"Maybe major construction here at the ranch to lure me back?"

"Nonsense, I know nothing about construction—just animals—dogs, cats, goats."

Jessie still believed Jordan was hiding something, but she decided to let it go. She'd never been able to get him to open up when he was a kid, and he was even more reticent now. Jessie wondered how Kat dealt with his secrets. She would ask her sister-in-law when they were alone.

"Okay, enough sightseeing. I want a beer and some nachos with *queso*," Jordan continued, "and I can smell that beef on the spit. Too bad it's too early in the year for corn on the cob, but I'm looking forward to Consuela's baked beans."

"You know, not everything we are serving today is organic," Matt said, referring to Jordan's preference for organic meat and produce. "Can you live with that?"

"Unless I want to go hungry or miss out on the best part of the meal, I guess I'll have to live with it."

They bickered harmlessly as they made their way back to the meadow where tables were set. People had been bringing food to add to the menu and the tables now groaned under the weight of pies and cakes, salads, and homemade breads. If anyone left Whitaker Ranch hungry, they had no one to blame but themselves.

Jessie looked around for her husband, who had mysteriously disappeared, and found him talking with Luis Largo. Maria Largo and their children were standing off to the side as if not certain where they should be.

"Welcome, Maria, and welcome to your children, as well," Jessie said, greeting the Largo family with a smile. "You must be so proud of the improvements Luis has accomplished for Matt here at the ranch."

Maria obviously took pride in her husband's success. The children spied some of their friends from school and ran off to play, but Maria still seemed hesitant to mingle and move into the festivities until she recognized a parent she knew.

Jessie went into the kitchen to let Consuela know that Maria had come. The two women were good friends. As Jessie went out the kitchen door she called over her shoulder, "I'll send some hands to carry the vat out to the dining area."

Consuela acknowledged with a *"Gracias, Señora,"* and then went to find Maria Largo. How wonderful to see old friends united, Jess thought.

MATT MOVED AROUND THE PICNIC AREA mingling with the guests and doing his best to make everyone feel welcome. He introduced himself to Jessie's professional associates and bragged on his wife's talent. He wanted them all to know he supported her career and her efforts to advance further into the world of professional illustrating.

Matt talked at length with one man, Bart Ayers, who introduced himself as a professional photographer.

"May I come back to the ranch another time to take photographs?" Bart asked. "I'm publishing a book about the fifty-three *Colorado Fourteeners*. Mt. Bierstadt, just to the northwest of here, is one of them," Ayers said, as if Matt wouldn't know that.

The two men had moved up a hill to enjoy

the perspective from Whitaker Ranch. It was different from what could be seen on the trails accessible to the public at the summit of Guanella Pass. Bart praised the beauty of the mountain as seen from their perch. They were engaged in a discussion of the merits of various cameras when Jessie interrupted.

"Matt, will you send a couple of strong men into Consuela's kitchen to move the vat of baked beans out to the picnic area?"

"Jess, you could ask the hands yourself. They will always do your bidding."

"You know I don't like to ask them to do chores of this sort. They are employees of the ranch, not my personal servants." She gave her husband a big smile as if begging his forgiveness for interrupting.

"I'll do it," Matt answered, "if you'll keep Bart entertained while I'm gone. I assume you two know each other?"

Bart spoke up. "No we haven't met. Mrs. Whitaker, I'm Bart Ayers. I came up with one of your guests. I begged for the opportunity to be her escort so I could look at the incredible vistas of Mt. Bierstadt as seen from your ranch. I hope to photograph it someday from your property."

Jessie reached out her hand in welcome, but

instead of shaking it, Bart lifted it to his lips. Matt wasn't particularly comfortable with this exchange, and Jessie raised her eyebrows as if to say "is this guy for real?"

"I better get some ranch hands to bring those beans out or Consuela will pour them over my head," Matt said as he reluctantly left the pair.

Jessie waved to her husband, then turned back to their guest. Matt heard her ask, "Which of my guests did you escort, Mr. Ayers?"

He didn't hear Ayers' reply, but hurried to get the requested task accomplished and return to his wife as quickly as possible. The photographer had seemed all right when the two of them were talking about photos and cameras, but now Matt wasn't so sure. He was uncomfortable leaving Jessie alone with the man, but it couldn't be helped. She was good at taking care of herself, and there were at least a hundred people at the foot of the hill.

Spying Jeremy, Matt stopped his brother-in-law. Pointing toward Jessie, he said, "Will you go up there and hang out with your sister?"

"Trouble?"

"I don't think so, but I left her in the company of a smarmy kind of fellow, and I would feel better if she had family at her side."

"What kind of word is smarmy? That's not a word I would expect you to use."

"In my mind, Jeremy, he is creepy and oily," Matt responded.

"On my way."

"Thanks, Jeremy."

Matt continued down the hill until he spotted his foreman. "Tom, grab another hand and move the vat of baked beans out of Consuela's kitchen to the picnic area. I guess we'll be eating soon."

"Will do, Boss."

When he returned, Matt heard Ayers ask Jeremy what he did for a living.

Jeremy had assumed a tough-guy persona. "I'm a trouble shooter, Bart. I freelance. I make problems go away."

"What kind of problems?" Ayers asked.

"The two-legged kind."

The color drained from the photographer's face. "Oh, I see my date. I should join her," he said, taking off down the hill.

Jessie struggled to keep from laughing out loud. "The two-legged kind? Oh, Jeremy, you are too much. I always knew you had delusions of grandeur."

"Well, I made that two-legged problem go away, didn't I?"

"You sure did," Matt confirmed.

The three linked arms and started down the hill toward the picnic area. The crowd was moving in that direction, as well.

The chuck wagon cooks sliced the beef from the carcass and mounded it high on serving platters. Another ranch hand ladled baked beans onto plates as guests passed by. Some of the local women had appointed themselves in charge of dishing out salads and breads. Plywood planks covered with canvas lay across sawhorses and served as tables. Many of the guests had brought lawn chairs, so everyone who wanted a seat was able to find one. A number of the men just stood holding their plates and shoveling in the grub.

The food wasn't fancy, but beef and beans had been the cuisine of choice in this part of the world for more than two centuries. Add some hot chilies to spice it up and no one would ask for anything different. This was the food of the High Country.

After everyone had been served and some had gone back for seconds, Matt stood up and called for everyone's attention.

"This gathering is for multiple purposes," he said, speaking loudly. "One of the reasons is to kick off the coming High Country spring and summer. Those seasons are too short at this altitude, so we need to enjoy every day we can. Another reason is to show off the improvements made here at Whitaker Ranch. We've finally moved into the twenty-first century. And the final reason is to celebrate the birthday of our beloved vet. Jordan, stand up so everybody can see you while we sing *Happy Birthday*."

The crowd sang with gusto while Jordan endured it with a red face. Kat planted a big kiss on his face while everybody cheered and clapped. Matt felt very satisfied with himself, but he could tell from the look on his brother-in-law's face that payback would be coming his way soon.

AFTER ALL THE OTHER GUESTS HAD BEEN SEEN safely on their way, Jordan, Kat, Jeremy, and Torrey joined Jessie and Matt in the great room at the back of the ranch house. Stretched out comfortably in the conversation area filled with overstuffed chairs and couches, the six of them discussed how successful the day had been and the fun they'd had.

"Torrey," Jessie said, "I barely caught sight of you today."

"That's because I was hanging out with people I haven't seen in a year or more." Torrey turned toward Matt. "Thank you for hosting this. The barbecue was a wonderful opportunity to reestablish friendships."

Suddenly it seemed everyone was thanking Matt. "I got to see my college buddies and show off my wife," Jordan said, "even if you did embarrass me by singing *Happy Birthday*. When I agreed to be the excuse for this gathering, I stressed no hoopla."

Something clicked in Jessie's mind. *If Jordan had been an excuse, what had been the real reason for the gathering? What did all the people in this room know that she didn't?*

Standing, Jessie excused herself, saying she would return in five minutes. When she left the room she positioned herself out of sight but not out of earshot. She intended to engage in some blatant eavesdropping.

Before long she heard her husband say, "Jordan, Kat, thanks for your discretion when Jessie was showing you around. I'm not certain how she might have reacted if she knew you had seen it all before and been involved in the planning."

"Is your relationship still strained? I thought

things were all patched up between you two," Torrey said. "It certainly looked that way today."

"You know Jess. She had her hostess face on today. Things have been good between us this last week, but I'm still on trial."

Hearing all she needed to hear, Jessie crept down the hall to the bedroom. She pulled off her jeans and shirt and slipped into a floor-length caftan.

Putting her hostess face back on, she returned to the great room. "Sorry, family, I needed to get into something comfortable. It has been a long day."

"We should go," Kat said, "and let you and Matt rest."

"Nonsense, don't go. We never have an opportunity for all of us just to hang together. And now that I'm living here on the ranch, I'll have even fewer opportunities to see you."

"That brings up another question," Jeremy said. "Matt, when are you going to replace Jessie's Rover? Are you waiting for the insurance settlement?"

"No," Matt said with a laugh. "I don't need to wait for the insurance settlement. We've just been busy this last week with preparations for the barbecue and we've had no time. Jess and I can go on the Internet tomorrow and order whatever she wants. We'll go through one of the dealerships in Lakewood or west Littleton so we don't have as far to go to take delivery."

"Sure wouldn't want to order it in east Aurora," Jeremy quipped. "That's half a state away."

The conversation turned to how metropolitan Denver had sprawled to the east and north and south, even climbing up the foothills to the west. Jessie tuned the conversation out.

In her own mind, she examined the evidence she had overheard. There was a conspiracy going on, and everyone in her family was involved. *Her accident apparently had thrown a monkey wrench into the timeline, but Matt had compensated.* She decided she was being herded, and she was about to dig in her heels.

Her train of thought was interrupted when Torrey asked, "Jess, how did you enjoy your stay in New York?"

Jessie considered before answering. She could be truthful and say she hated it, but that would just give the other side additional ammunition. "The visit was very worthwhile. I made a number of valuable contacts. In fact, now that I'm finished with the bulk of the work for the Colorado Convention and Visitors Bureau, I'm going to send some sample sketches to a few writers and agents I met during my stay."

She talked animatedly about the places she'd visited, the people she'd met, and how different the culture was in the Big Apple.

"It took me a while to sort out the numbered streets and numbered avenues," she admitted ruefully. "I got turned around more than once. And it didn't help that some streets had more than one name. Avenue of the Americas and Sixth Avenue were names for the same street in midtown. I took cabs everywhere because I was afraid to ride the subway."

When she finally wound down, Jessie realized her family was looking at her with concern. "Oh, wow! I got carried away, didn't I?"

"I think you got too many stimuli today," Torrey said. "Now I know we need to go and let you unwind."

As they all rose to leave, Jessie called out, "Wait, you can't go yet. I have CARE packages to send home with you."

She came back from the kitchen with containers filled with barbecue beef, baked beans, and assorted desserts. The largest she gave to

Kat, and then she gave smaller ones to Torrey and Jeremy.

"Hey, why does Kat get a bigger carton than me?" Jeremy objected.

"Because there are two of them, there is only one of you. And yours is bigger than Torrey's because you're a bottomless pit."

"Go home, Jeremy," Matt said. "You're driving your sister to the edge."

With hugs and kisses and promises of getting together soon, everyone left. Jeremy and Torrey rode down the road with Jordan and Kat.

Jessie felt wrung out and didn't have the stamina to take on Matt tonight. Turning on her heel, she tossed over her shoulder, "I'm tired. I'm going to bed." She stalked away.

She heard Matt come into the bedroom but she feigned sleep. There would be no loving tonight.

EIGHT

Jessie slept late the next morning, but even so, she woke in a foul mood. She didn't really feel as if she had gotten any rest. Her head ached and her stomach was upset. Most importantly, she didn't know what to do about the situation between her and Matt.

She knew it would be deceitful, but she needed to play nice with her husband until her Rover had been replaced.

Right now, she was a virtual prisoner because without transportation of her own, she couldn't even get down to Spruce Creek, much less farther away. She could walk to the bottom of the ranch road, but the pass wouldn't be opened until Memorial Day, so it wasn't as if she could thumb a ride on the highway. There was no traffic yet.

She decided she shouldn't feel any guilt about misleading Matt. He and her entire family had deceived her since she'd returned from the East Coast. She was on her own. She didn't have anyone she could conspire with.

Groaning, she rolled out of bed and headed for the shower. It was obvious Matt had showered early because the steam in the bathroom had dissipated even though there was a damp towel on the rack. She briefly thought perhaps she should lounge in the Whirlpool instead of showering but decided she needed coffee more than a soak in the tub. Still, she took her time, not in any hurry to confront her husband.

Jessie and Matt were on their own for breakfast. Sunday was Consuela's day off. She and two Catholic ranch hands left early to drive to Bailey for Sunday mass. Jess knew Consuela then spent the rest of the day with her sister and came back up to the ranch in the evening. She didn't know what the ranch hands did on Sunday to keep busy—they, too, probably had family to visit. But the arrangement had been going on for years so it obviously worked for all concerned.

Walking into the kitchen, Jessie was relieved to find coffee ready to brew and a breakfast casserole that just needed to be zapped in the microwave. Matt had invested in a Keurig shortly after she had returned from New York. Drinking the fresh brewed coffee while staying at her house apparently convinced him the Keurig was perfect.

She slid the breakfast meal into the microwave, knowing Matt had made the casserole—a concoction of beaten eggs, bell pepper, onions, and hash brown potatoes. Consuela wouldn't have had time before she'd left the ranch. Jessie had to give Matt points for trying. But she would make her own decision about staying in their marriage.

She heard Matt coming and decided she would be civil. She wouldn't give anything away. Not knowing what she knew would keep him from maneuvering circumstances to convince her she was wrong about the conspiracy.

"Hi, honey," she greeted him. "Thanks for making the casserole. It looks delicious, and I'm happy I didn't have to find something to cook for breakfast."

Matt looked relieved, which told Jessie he'd not been certain what to expect from her this morning. Relaxing, he asked if after breakfast she would be ready to go car shopping. She nodded her agreement.

After rinsing the breakfast dishes and slipping them into the dishwasher, Jessie followed her husband into his office. Matt logged onto the Internet. He obviously had been practicing. He expertly surfed for all-wheel-drive vehicles. Ultimately, Jessie decided she wanted another Range Rover. Hers had withstood the impact of the deer, had not veered out of control, and had been responsible for her coming home with a minimum number of minor injuries.

Matt went to the manufacturer's website and placed the order for the model Jessie wanted with exact specifications for extras.

"Jessie, you know it'll be a few weeks before the Rover is ready. But you may take mine—if I'm unable to drive you—anytime you want to go down to Spruce Creek.

Jessie hugged Matt because she believed that's what she would have done if she'd been unaware of his treacherous plot to keep her on the ranch.

Telling her husband she planned to hang out in her studio for a few hours, she wandered down the walkway and into her space. She hadn't bothered to lock her door because she had been showing people about the studio all during the barbecue. Their guests were friends. No one would abuse her trust. But some things had been disturbed in her office. Items on her desk weren't exactly as she had left them. She quickly moved across the anteroom to the studio area. Things there were disturbed also.

After finding nothing missing, she decided some of the children had wandered in and, being kids, had shuffled through stuff. Satisfied she had solved that minor mystery, she put it from her mind. She had more important things to think about. Running away from Matt obviously didn't work. He'd told her the major decision hanging between the two of them would be hers to make. He had made the ranch accessible, and he'd made it possible for her to work and have privacy. She did love him. But she hated being maneuvered. She would get the upper hand. She began plotting revenge against her husband and her brothers.

MATT WASN'T SURE WHAT TO THINK ABOUT Jessie's reactions. She was saying and doing all the right things, but something was amiss—it was as if she were acting a part. He was certain a tactical error had been made somewhere along the way. He sat at his desk and reviewed his strategy. He'd made the ranch accessible. He'd established first class communications with the outside world. He'd provided Jessie with privacy and working space.

Their lovemaking had been frequent and passionate, except for last night. Maybe she'd been truly tired. But he knew she hadn't been asleep when he came to bed. She'd been faking it, but he wasn't sure why. She simply could have said she didn't want to make love.

He needed to go back to courting her. He had been treating Jessie as a wife, not a lover. He would cook dinner tonight and serve it by candlelight. They would have a fine Merlot. Wine always relaxed her. Then he would give her the bracelet that matched the Concho necklace. If it weren't Sunday, he could have one of the hands bring back a bouquet of roses, but there would be no florists open today in a small town like Bailey.

Better yet, he would take her out to dinner. He would still give her the jewelry at dinner, but going out would be more romantic than eating at the ranch.

He wandered through the house looking for her when he remembered she'd planned to work in her studio. Observing her privacy, he made a habit of not going to her studio unless invited, so instead he picked up the phone and called her.

"Jess, I've a wonderful idea. How about we dress in our finest and go into Denver for dinner and a night on the town. You've been cooped up here at the ranch, and you deserve a real night out."

Matt waited, breath held. It seemed as if it took Jessie a long time to consider the invitation.

"Okay, what time would you want to leave?"

"If we left here at five thirty, we should be able to make a seven o'clock reservation."

"Thank you, Matt. I'll be ready."

Matt was even more confused. Jessie had said all the right words, but she hadn't seemed particularly enthusiastic. It was as if she were accepting an invitation to a business lunch.

Matt phoned Elway's in Cherry Creek. Having telephone service really was convenient. He wondered why he ever did without it.

He was able to get reservations for seven o'clock without difficulty. He told the hostess they were celebrating a special occasion—he and his wife were on their honeymoon. He alerted the restaurant he would want a bottle of *Taittinger Cuvee Prestige* and asked for a corsage if it could be arranged.

Traffic would be relatively heavy going into

Denver, weekenders returning home in preparation for the workweek. But coming back to the ranch there should be little, if any, traffic. He'd restrict himself to a single glass of champagne since he'd be the one behind the wheel—but that would mean Jessie could have as much as she wanted. He didn't plan on getting his wife drunk, exactly, but he hoped she would be very relaxed.

At four o'clock, he went into the bathroom to shower and shave. When he came out, Jessie was in their walk-in closet selecting a dress. While she'd been in New York, she'd acquired a few attractive cocktail dresses—dresses he wanted to be sure she would have an opportunity to wear.

She pulled out two and held them up for his inspection. "Which one?" she asked.

Matt looked critically at the two dresses. He suspected this was some kind of a test. "The green," he said decisively. He knew he couldn't afford to sound uncertain.

"Good choice," Jessie responded. "I can wear the green turquoise Concho necklace with this dress. Would you like that?"

"I'd like that a whole lot," Matt said, thinking of his planned gift of the matching bracelet.

He watched as Jessie went through the

female ritual of preparing for a big date. She was so beautiful, and he took great pleasure in admiring her body as she dressed.

She slipped into lacy panties and bra, and then she draped the silky green dress over her head and shoulders, letting it slip into place. She turned her back to Matt for him to pull the zipper closed.

He thought he would rather be moving the zipper in the opposite direction. That would be his goal later in the evening.

Jessie sat at her dressing table and skillfully applied her makeup. Matt was amazed that a bit of this and a dab of that could turn her from Jessie, the fresh-faced country girl, into Jessica, a seductive temptress.

Before fastening the Concho necklace she handed him, he leaned down and gave her a kiss on her sexy neck.

They walked out the front door of the ranch house at exactly five-thirty.

WHEN THEY DID ARRIVE AT THE RESTAURANT, the parking lot was almost empty and they found a space close to the front door. Even though they were a few minutes early, they were seated right away, a gesture Matt appreciated. The hostess greeted them with a friendly smile and led them to their table.

Jessie had not been to Elway's before, and Matt watched her as she almost choked at the prices on the menu. Matt removed it from her hands and laid it face down on the table. He could imagine what she was thinking—*Thank God my husband is rich.*

"Trust me," Matt said. "I'll order for you."

She nodded her acquiescence.

When the waiter arrived, Matt said, "We'll both start with the lobster cocktail, followed by your black bean soup. For an entrée, the lady will have Colorado rack of lamb with sautéed asparagus. I'll have the roasted Alaskan halibut and twice-baked potato."

"Very good, sir, and what do you wish to drink?"

"*Taittinger Cuvee Prestige.* I reserved a bottle when I made our dinner reservations."

"Ah, yes, and you also requested flowers, I believe." Matt watched as the waiter turned away and went to speak with the hostess. Soon, she arrived at their table with an exquisite white orchid corsage, which she handed to Matt.

He thanked the hostess. Then Matt bent to pin the corsage to Jessie's dress, nuzzling her ear as he did so.

"Matt," she whispered, "you're making me suspicious again. What have you done that I deserve all of this?"

"As I told you the last time you asked that question, I'm guilty of taking you for granted, and I'm trying to change my ways. I'm courting you."

When the champagne arrived and their glasses had been filled, Matt proposed a toast. "To our honeymoon. May it last forever." After they had sipped the wine, he pulled the jewelry box from his inside coat pocket and handed it to Jessie. "Something to go with your necklace."

She sucked in her breath as she beheld the matching liquid silver and green turquoise bracelet. She held out her arm for Matt to fasten the bracelet on her wrist. "Thank you, Matt. You are incredibly generous. But I hope you don't think you must buy my love. It is given freely."

He tried to articulate his thoughts. "I'd never try to buy your love. I have too much respect for you. But look at me—I'm the luckiest man in this restaurant just because I have you at my side," he said as he glanced around the restaurant to prove his point. "I want to give you beautiful things because you are beautiful." He stretched out his hand and gently squeezed hers. "I want to take you places because you make me look good."

Taking her hand, he said, "It doesn't matter how much money I have. The only worthwhile thing I've ever done in my life is love you. If you love me in return, it isn't because of anything I've done or anything I've given you. If you love me, it is because you are incredibly generous, and you have given me the most precious commodity in the world."

"Matt, I . . ." Before she could say anything more, the waiter appeared with the lobster cocktails. He lingered to make certain everything was satisfactory, and he topped off Jessie's glass with more champagne. The moment was lost.

Their conversation became less intense as they enjoyed their dinner. They talked about music and the theater while they slowly ate, savoring both food and ambiance.

Matt took special gratification in watching Jessie enjoy her meal. He thought she was enjoying an orgasmic experience while she was eating her rack of lamb, the pleasure on her face was so intense. He knew how much she loved it, and at Elway's it was always prepared perfectly. Of course, she also had her much-loved asparagus. Matt wondered if asparagus could be grown in a greenhouse. He would find out. The Internet would have the answer.

When the waiter had cleared their table, he inquired if they wished dessert. Matt was certain neither of them could swallow another bite so he declined, but he did order coffee. When the waiter lifted the champagne bottle to pour more, Matt waved him away. Jessie had consumed two and a half glasses. He didn't want her hating herself in the morning because of a hangover, or worse, hating him because he had encouraged her to overindulge. They both had swallowed enough champagne. It wasn't necessary to empty the bottle.

Matt smiled at the waiter's surprise. Few diners would leave behind a third of a bottle of expensive champagne. He knew their waiter would cork it and share it in the kitchen after the restaurant closed. Matt considered it just another tip for good service.

The waiter brought their coffee and the check. When he returned with the credit slip for a signature, Matt laid a fifty-dollar bill on the tray in place of adding a tip to the bill. He didn't think waiters should lose a percentage of their tips to a merchant account fee.

As they left the restaurant for the drive home, Matt hoped his wife would let him make love with her tonight.

JESSIE COULDN'T RESTRAIN HER ANGER ANY longer. Tonight had just been another instance of her husband's manipulative behavior. Matt had obviously intended to placate her with dinner and more jewelry.

And her brother . . . the scene in Jordan's office came to mind. Talking about whelps and herd dogs—*hogwash*. The two of them had been plotting to get her to the ranch and keep her there. The discussion between her brothers and Matt after their guests had left the previous night told her Torrey and Kat had been in on the plot too. Her entire family was in league against her.

"Matt," she spoke up, "I want to move to Denver."

"What?" he asked, sounding surprised but keeping his eyes on the road.

"You and my family are plotting to keep me a prisoner on the ranch. You all think you know what is best for me—that I'm too dimwitted to lead my own life—that I need supervision. I'm tired of being herded, of being manipulated. It's going to end."

Jessie paused for a breath. She'd been betrayed by all those she loved and trusted. She just couldn't see a successful resolution. Matt was too controlling, and her brothers took his side. There could be no reconciliation between them.

"Jess, listen to me," Matt pleaded. "It's true we plotted to get you to the ranch, that the barbeque for Jordan's birthday was planned as an event you wouldn't be able to refuse. But it was only because I didn't believe there was any other way I'd get you to come up and see the changes."

Jessie was surprised when Matt pulled off to the side of the road and took her hands in his.

"I needed to show you that you can live at the ranch and still have everything you want career-wise. I don't want the ranch to be your prison. I want it to be your home." Matt's eyes locked onto hers. "Please, Jess, don't leave me."

He had been manipulating, but without malicious intent. Realizing how foolish she was being, she stared back at Matt. "Take me home, husband."

NINE

The day came when Jessie and Matt were to pick up her new Range Rover. A clerk at the dealership had phoned two days earlier telling them the vehicle had arrived and, as soon as the dealer prep was finished, she could take possession.

Matt tried to talk her into waiting until after the long weekend, but without success. She knew west-bound traffic into the mountains would be heavy on the Thursday before Memorial Day, but she didn't care. She was anxious to have her own transportation.

Jessie and Matt left the ranch early in the morning, hoping to get the transaction completed and start back before noon.

She was excited. Life on the ranch was

bucolic, so there were few occasions to mark the passage of time. Even a trip to Littleton was an adventure. Jessie admitted to herself that, once she got her sense of betrayal off her chest, she hadn't felt restricted or confined on the ranch. Matt's Rover was available to her most of the time, even if she didn't use it. She could come and go as she pleased. And he always invited her to join him when he was going to Spruce Creek or Grant. But surprisingly, she found she was content at most times to stay working in her studio.

Since the barbecue, she had picked up a commission directly from an author to illustrate a new children's book. The author emailed her each chapter as it was finished and, for the most part, allowed Jessie to submit whatever illustrations she thought appropriate. Occasionally, the author would make suggestions, but overall she was very easy to work with.

If the book sold, Jessie would receive part of the advance and continuing royalties. The project wouldn't make her rich, but it would get her name and illustrations in front of other potential clients.

Today promised to be full of adventure. She chattered at Matt as they started out. The drive from the ranch was a pleasure. The roads were dry, the air was warm and sweet, and the only patches of snow in sight were in the dark pockets where the sun never reached. Rocky Mountain columbine and other wild flowers dotted the side of the highway in those places where the forest didn't intrude.

It seemed that, before she knew it, they were out of the foothills that butted up against the Front Range. Jessie admitted to herself she didn't miss the hustle and bustle of city life. Littleton may have been considered a suburb of Denver, but it was not a bedroom community. There was plenty of commercial activity on its major thoroughfares.

She felt slightly apprehensive as Matt pulled into the dealership parking lot. She hadn't driven since the accident. But she was certain she would be fine as soon as they were out of town and on the highway.

When they walked into the showroom, a salesperson rushed up to help them. As soon as Matt explained why they had come, the salesman called for the manager and walked away.

"No need to spend time on people who won't earn him a commission," Jessie muttered.

When the Rover was brought to the pick-up

area, Matt went over it with a fine-toothed comb. Jessie understood, since the only money the dealership would make off this transaction was the prep charge. They weren't too concerned with customer satisfaction.

When he was satisfied, Matt went to the cashier and paid the necessary fees. Jessie followed after him.

Matt suggested she let him drive her new Rover to the nearest gas station for a fill up. Jessie thought that was a great idea. Driving his Rover, Jessie tailed behind Matt and her new vehicle to a station two blocks away on Wadsworth Boulevard. Matt filled her Rover's gas tank and then his. They switched vehicles, and Matt gave her last minute instructions.

"I want you to go first. With a new vehicle you never know what can happen. If I'm following you, I'll see if you get into trouble."

In spite of her trepidation, Jessie didn't want Matt to know she was nervous about driving again. "I'll be okay, Matt. But I intend to drive the speed limit so don't get impatient traveling behind me."

Jessie relaxed. She felt fine once she was out on the highway and away from cross-town traffic. The Rover was a little stiff, but it was new and needed to be broken in. She wasn't in any hurry. They left town well before noon, so traffic wasn't any worse than any other Thursday. There were passing lanes on Highway 285 so travelers in a hurry could get by her without risk. She felt good to be driving again.

They stopped at the clinic when they got to Spruce Creek. Jessie wanted to show off her new Range Rover. Torrey and Kat were properly appreciative. But Jordan was very ho-hum. Jeremy wasn't in town, but had he been, he would probably be as unexcited as Jordan. When they waved goodbye, they were looking forward to Consuela's lunch.

Jessie was relieved when she turned onto the ranch road. It was pleasant to drive twenty-five miles an hour up to the ranch house. Five miles an hour had always been a trial and made the last part of the trip seem endless. She'd just come around a curve before starting up the steepest stretch when she saw a sports car in front of her. It appeared to be in trouble. No one in their right mind would drive a sports car on this road into the back country.

Jessie stopped and, staying in her car, waited for Matt to catch up with her. When he did, he pulled behind her. Getting out of his vehicle and seeing why she had stopped, he returned to the Rover and unlocked his Remington 30-06 from the overhead gun rack.

"STAY HERE," MATT SAID TO JESSIE AS HE passed her. Striding up the hill like Daniel Boone, he approached the stranded car. It was hung up on a high center.

Seeing the rifle in Matt's hand, the two men froze. Matt could see fear on their faces. "You're on private property. I don't suppose you saw the *No Trespassing* sign at the entrance to my road?"

"Uh, no, sir," the smaller of the two men spoke up. "We thought this was a Forest Service road. We're just looking for a camping spot."

Matt could see his *No Trespassing* sign on the back seat. "That's why you have so much camping gear in your tiny sports car, right?" he asked sarcastically.

"We're just scouting out a spot. We didn't plan on camping tonight."

"Jess," Matt yelled, "drive around us. Go up to the ranch and send Tom and Manuel and Skip down here. We'll need some beef to pick up this little car and turn it around." He asked for the three biggest men at the ranch so he'd enjoy the intimidation factor, as well.

Jessie started her Rover and squeezed past the strangers' vehicle.

Matt knew she would fully brief his foreman, Tom, and the two other hands before letting them start down to where he waited. Jessie might be stubborn on occasion, like insisting they go into town today, but she was no dummy.

Matt rested against a large rock and let the barrel of the Remington dip toward the ground so it was no longer pointed directly at the men. But if one of them so much as scratched, the rifle would be sighted on him immediately.

He relaxed a little when he saw the big truck come over the rise and start down the hill. Tom stopped about fifteen feet away from where Matt and the trespassers were located. Tom was wearing a sidearm and his other two men were carrying rifles.

"Stand at the rear of the car, gentlemen," Matt instructed the intruders.

"Tom, pat them down, make certain they aren't armed."

After doing as instructed, Tom said, "They're clean, Boss."

"Okay, check the registration, record the

license number and the VIN, then check their driver's licenses."

Moving carefully, not straying between the armed ranch hands and the two trespassers, Tom did as Matt instructed. "This car isn't registered to either of these two, Boss. It's registered to a Shirley Rossiter. This guy's name is Ralph Polanski and the other one is Leo Gutes."

"It belongs to my little sister," the larger man, Leo, spoke for the first time. "Really, mister, we haven't done nothing wrong."

"Are you saying you haven't done anything wrong?" Matt asked correcting the guy's English. "Except tear down a sign, trespass on private property, and probably tear out the oil pan on your sister's car. You realize even if we turn this car around, you won't be able to drive out of here? The engine would seize up before you got to Spruce Creek."

"Tom, take Manuel with you and escort Leo up to the ranch in the truck," Matt told his foreman with a look of disgust. "Skip and I'll escort the little guy, Ralph. When I get there, I'll call the sheriff and ask him to run the license number to see if the car is stolen and if there are any wants and warrants on these two bozos. If not, then Leo can call his sister and tell her he damaged her car. He can also call for a flatbed tow truck. The sheriff will know where to find the nearest one. I don't think there's one based in Grant."

Matt had Leo and Ralph sit out on the front porch. He called into the house for Jessie to bring him the phone. After talking with the sheriff and learning that Ralph and Leo probably were what they appeared to be—a couple of schmucks on a joy ride—he had the hands rack their rifles, and he locked his Remington back in the Range Rover.

Leo had a short but painful phone conversation with his sister. From time to time Matt could hear her yelling, and what she was saying wasn't complimentary. She called her brother every name in the book and even a few Matt hadn't heard before.

When that ordeal was over, Matt took the phone back and called Hank at Fueling Stop and Snacks. It turned out the State Patrol contracted with a guy in Grant for vehicle rescue services. The sheriff had told Matt that Hank knew how to reach him, and if he wasn't already on a tow he would come up. He didn't come cheap, but Matt assured the sheriff he wasn't the one paying.

Hank told Matt the tow truck driver would

call him back. Sure enough, in less than five minutes the phone rang and Rupert was on the line. After telling him where the vehicle was located, Rupert said it would be an hour and a half to two hours before he could get there, but he would call when he was on his way. Then Matt put Leo on the phone to work out his own payment arrangements.

Taking pity on the two bozos, and because his own stomach was growling, Matt brought them into the kitchen where they sat down to a meal of beans and tortillas. Consuela put out cheese, peppers, and onions they could add to their beans as they wished. She poured iced tea and asked if anyone wanted anything more. When there were no takers, she went to her own room.

"Okay," Matt said, "let's have the truth. What were you guys really looking for?"

After sharing a look with his buddy, Ralph spoke up. "We heard there was a pot farm up this way."

Matt couldn't help himself; he started laughing, "Not on my land, there isn't. And I doubt if there are any on the adjacent Forest Service land, at least not on this side of the Divide. I've heard of them finding some on the Western Slope." Understanding dawned on Matt.

"No wonder you guys were scared shitless—you thought I was a pot grower. If I had been, you would probably be dead. I hear the growers dislike trespassers even more than ranchers do."

When Rupert called, Matt drove them back down to their car. He was very glad to see the last of them. But the incident reminded him it was time to prepare for the onset of summer tourists.

THE MEMORIAL DAY WEEKEND WENT BY WITH no more unwanted visitors. Matt had driven down to the entrance of the ranch road on Friday and posted a large wooden sign which said *Private Property – Trespassers Will Be Shot!* Then about every quarter mile up the ranch road, and all along Guanella Pass Road where it abutted the ranch property, he posted signs saying *No Hunting! No Fishing! No Trespassing! Violators Will Be Shot!*

When Jessie teased Matt about being antisocial, he became defensive. "Honey, if I shoot somebody, I don't want them to be able to claim they weren't warned. Ever since they paved the highway from the top of the pass down to Georgetown, we're getting more yahoos on this side just looking for trouble."

Knowing when it was best to retreat, Jessie said, "I'm sure you're right, honey," and gave him a hug.

Since Matt had improved the ranch road, it was more attractive to hikers, campers, and families looking for picnic sites. So, in reality, it was a good thing Matt had gone on the offensive to deter people from intruding. Jessie had been frightened by the episode on Thursday and was secretly happy Matt had reacted the way he had. She just wouldn't tell him she approved.

Every time she praised him for being protective, he became even more so. He had gotten to the point where he was even suggesting she go nowhere unless she took one of the ranch hands with her. When she pointed out that, even if Thursday's trespassers had been dangerous in some way, she had never been in danger because she had stopped well away from them and she never left the vehicle, Matt finally conceded she was right.

They rubbed along in harmonious companionship through the month of June. They attended the church wedding and reception held for Jordan and Kat—Kat told Jessie she had decided she didn't want to wait until fall. Jessie got to meet Kat's family—her parents and brother.

Jessie and Matt rode horseback to the top of the Continental Divide. They picnicked in the high meadows above the tree line.

For the Fourth of July, they went to the big Independence Day celebration in Breckenridge. Matt participated in a 10K run. They enjoyed a big breakfast while they watched the Main Street Parade. They listened to a rock concert in the afternoon and a spirited patriotic orchestra performance in the evening. They spent the night in a romantic bed and breakfast.

July passed with anticipation of the arrival of the newest member of the Walker family. Jessie talked to Kat on the phone every day, getting a read on how she was feeling. She was just happy it was Kat and not her who was expecting.

Matt's frequent lovemaking was bliss to Jessie. She knew physically she could never get enough of her husband. He fulfilled her every need. She also knew she was falling deeper in love with him, if that were possible. But there were still unresolved issues in their marriage that she didn't know how to deal with.

Jessie woke one morning feeling bilious. Matt was already up and gone from their bed. So after she showered and dressed, she went in search of him.

"Matt," she called out when she found him, "come in and have breakfast with me." She really didn't want to eat, but she wanted to be with her husband, and she needed an excuse that wouldn't make her appear clingy in front of the ranch hands.

"Honey, I can't right now. I have new stock arriving today, and we need to get the corral ready."

Jessie felt herself tearing up. This was ridiculous. She almost never cried and certainly not because her husband didn't have time for her.

She heard Tom say, "Go ahead, Boss, we've got this," as he nodded toward a couple of the hands.

Matt joined her. "I've already eaten, but I'll drink a cup of coffee while you eat. What do you want to talk about?"

"Do you love me?" Jessie whimpered.

"Of course I love you, you silly goose. Jess, what's wrong?"

"I'm tired all the time. I'm not getting enough exercise. I'm spending too much time in front of my computer so I'm gaining weight. I'm just feeling down."

"You know what you need?" her husband replied. "You need some girl time. Call Torrey and set something up."

Matt was right, she decided. She needed a spa vacation.

Jessie phoned Torrey with the idea of her and Kat joining her at The Broadmoor in Colorado Springs. They could drive down one morning in the middle of the week, spend one night and two days being pampered, and come home late in the afternoon of the second day. She was disappointed when she learned that, because of her advanced pregnancy, Kat wouldn't be able to come, but perhaps it was just as well. Jessie could talk more freely with Torrey if Kat wasn't there. Torrey had taken the place of the mother who'd abandoned Jessie and her siblings when Jessie was only ten. Torrey knew Jessie better than any other person alive.

Arrangements were quickly made. Such things were easy when one's husband was wealthy and money was no object. So, one Tuesday morning in late August Jessie drove down to Spruce Creek, picked up Torrey, and they were off to The Broadmoor. The two-hour drive allowed the women to catch up on what was happening in each of their lives.

Jessie suspected Torrey sensed she was troubled about something when her questions became directed toward emotional issues. Jessie needed to focus on her driving, so she asked Torrey to postpone the touchy-feely conversation until they had settled into their suite at the resort. It wouldn't do to burst into tears while on a curvy mountain road.

When they arrived, it was too early to check in, so they enjoyed a terrific lunch of light pasta primavera with fresh fruit for dessert. They left their luggage with the bellman, who promised their bags would be placed into their suite as soon as it was available. Meanwhile, Jessie and Torrey enjoyed a soothing massage.

Jessie was totally relaxed when the two women finally went to their suite. She stretched out on a chaise lounge with her feet up, ready to confess all to Torrey. "Which problems do you want to hear about—the physical, mental, or emotional?"

"All of the above. Start with your physical problems. What are your symptoms?"

"I'm tired. I know part of the problem is I've gained weight. Consuela's cooking is just too tasty. For years I never ate three meals a day, and now I'm hungry and eating all the time."

"And mentally what's wrong?" Torrey asked.

"I can't stay focused. My mind wanders, and when I should be thinking about one thing, I'm thinking about another."

"What about your emotions?"

"That's the worst. Little things bring tears to my eyes. And I'm emotionally distraught trying to decide what to do about my marriage."

"Are you and Matt having problems? Is he being pushy and overbearing?"

"If we were having problems, it would be easier to understand my issues. As for being pushy, he is anything but. Torrey, I love him so much, but I don't know if I can stay married to him."

"Why's that?"

"After raising my brothers, I don't think I want children. I don't want to raise another family. Matt does, of course. But he says it's up to me to decide. I don't know if I can."

"I think you already have, Jess—I think you already have."

TEN

Other than missing her in his bed the previous night, Matt didn't think he was lonely as a result of Jessie's absence. This was the first time they had been apart since her accident in early May. He didn't have to like it, but he accepted she needed some time away on her own. He'd noticed she'd been moody lately, so maybe a couple of days away doing girlie things with Torrey would cheer her up. Besides which, she would be home this evening.

There was too much work needing to be done at this season of year for Matt to spend time manipulating Jessie. And he wasn't fooling her, so there wasn't much point in trying.

Matt knew he could leave the ranch work to his crew, but he liked to get his hands dirty. His foreman had known in May when to move the goats up from winter pasture. Tom also knew which goats were happiest working for what residents, and which residents asked for the same goats year after year, and which herds should go where on the Forest Service and BLM lands. His customers knew that letting goats do what they did best—eat—was the best deterrent available to prevent grass fires in mountain meadows. Matt could sit back and do nothing more than approve expenditures and pay bills. He could play at being a gentleman rancher, but he'd die of boredom.

Who'd have thought renting goats in the summer would be a viable business? Not especially lucrative, but viable. There wasn't enough profit to support him and a family—good thing he was rich and didn't need it—but there was enough to break even after paying the hands and the vet bills. Nice getting a family discount from the vet.

Next, he planned to expand his horse breeding and training program. He'd already brought some new stock in and he planned on getting more. But meanwhile, he needed work to keep him busy.

In spite of doing his best not to think about Jessie, he admitted he was concerned about her.

He knew she wasn't entirely happy on the ranch, no matter that he had negated all her objections to living beyond civilization. He had brought civilization here.

Maybe the ranch wasn't the problem; maybe Jessie wasn't happy living with him. He gave her the space she seemed to need. He didn't try to manage her, and their sex life was healthy and satisfying. What more could she want?

Courtship had slipped by the wayside. Since the Independence Day trip, he'd not done much for her that was special—just a picnic or two. He needed to get creative again—flowers, chocolates, more jewelry, some pretty clothes. He also needed to reassure Jessie again and again that children could wait until she was ready.

He understood why she didn't want to start a family now. She had already spent eighteen years of her life raising children. Torrey had been there to help, but ultimately it was Jessie who'd fixed breakfast every day for her father and brothers; made certain homework was done; that they all had clean clothes for school and work. She never had a childhood of her own. She'd gone to work right out of high school so her brothers could go to college. Fortunately, they'd both received scholarships, but Jessie's earnings had helped fill in the cracks.

Matt also understood Jessie was afraid she would discover child-rearing was just too much for her and that she would abandon her family in the same way her mother had—just up and walk away, never to be seen again. No phone calls. No letters. Nothing.

Matt knew that would never happen. Jessie had never walked away from a responsibility in her entire life. No matter how hard, no matter how distasteful, she stuck it out and finished what she started. That was why Matt didn't believe she would ever divorce him. She wasn't a quitter.

When he realized he had been standing for fifteen minutes doing nothing but thinking, he straightened his shoulders and told himself to get back to work. He tossed his tools into the big ranch truck, and then climbed in and started down the road. There was timber downed last winter he could haul up and split. They might not require burning fireplaces for warmth, but he loved the ambiance and was willing to do the work so he could enjoy a blazing fire in the evenings.

He drove all the way down to Guanella Pass Road and turned the truck around. He planned to work his way up the road, pulling the felled trees up onto the truck bed. He had a wench so the job wasn't really all that difficult.

He hadn't gone a mile up the road before he spotted a likely deadfall. He angled the truck across the road so the bed was in a straight line with the conifer he had in mind. He hopped down from the cab, pulled on his gloves, and dragged the heavy line toward the tree.

Wishing he had worn chaps, he waded through underbrush at the side of the road before scrambling down to where his target lay. He would have preferred a downed tree on the uphill side of the road, but he would take what he could get.

He wrapped the line around the trunk a few times and secured it. Then he scrambled back up to start the wench, and began pulling the tree up the hill. The tree hung up on a rock and the wench started screaming. Matt dropped it into neutral and worked his way down the line to clear the hang-up. After prying the offending rock out of the way, he once again returned to the truck and put the wench into gear.

He turned away to shift to a safer location, but he hadn't entirely moved out of its path when the line snapped. The heavy rope flew back and struck him in the back of the head, knocking him to his knees. He dragged himself to his feet and managed to shut down the wench before he collapsed, unconscious, on the road.

FIRST THING IN THE MORNING, JESSIE GAVE Torrey her car keys and asked her to find a nearby pharmacy and buy three different home pregnancy test kits. Jessie didn't trust just one. If she had two tests and got different results, she wanted a tie-breaker—hence the instructions to buy three. Jessie wouldn't go herself because she was afraid someone she knew would see her.

Torrey laughed at her paranoia, since the likelihood of seeing anyone she knew here in Colorado Springs was extremely small. But she did as her friend requested.

Jessie paced back and forth in the suite while she waited for Torrey to return. She was tempted to bite her fingernails, but she didn't. She wished she smoked, because she'd heard smoking soothed the nerves. She wanted a stiff drink, but if she were pregnant she wouldn't be drinking alcohol again anytime soon. So she poured her nervousness into pacing.

"What took you so long?" were the very first

words out of her mouth when Torrey came through the door.

"Jess, I've only been gone thirty minutes. Relax, child, whatever the results, they will not be changed by a few minutes' delay. They will be what they will be."

"Torrey, I'm so scared. What am I supposed to do?"

"Each test is a bit different. But they all require contact with urine. The results are based on hormones in your pee. Choose a box, go into the bathroom, read the instructions, take the test, and wait for the results. I think the results are ready in three minutes."

Jessie picked up the one labeled *First Response* and entered the bathroom. Five minutes later she came out. "Torrey, it shows two lines. That means I'm pregnant. What am I going to do?"

"You're going to take a second test to confirm the accuracy of the first."

"I don't think I can pee again right now."

"Then sit down and drink a couple of glasses of water." Emphasizing her words, Torrey filled a glass from the bottled water in the suite's little refrigerator. She handed the glass to Jessie. "Drink," she instructed.

Accustomed to doing what Torrey said since

she was the closest person to a mother she ever had, Jessie accepted the glass and emptied it.

When she started to pace again, Torrey engaged her in conversation. "When was your last period? Do you remember?"

Jessie focused on thinking of the correct answer. "It was in June, I think. Yes, I'm certain my last period was sometime in June. Oh, God, I missed my July period."

"What kind of contraceptives are you using? Or are you depending on Matt?"

"I'm using a vaginal ring. It's not that I don't trust Matt, but I think a woman should be responsible for her own body. I know I placed a new ring after my June period, but it may have been past its expiration date. I don't remember checking. I was late removing it in July and I got off schedule. If I'm pregnant, I need to remove it immediately."

"I think you can probably wait until you get a second positive on a home pregnancy test."

"I'm ready, I can pee now," Jessie said, grabbing a box labeled *Clearblue* and disappearing into the bathroom again.

Five minutes later she was back. "Okay, there's no doubt. I'm pregnant. This one gave me a plus sign. No need to use the third one."

"I'm sure we can return it," Torrey said, "since it hasn't been opened and I have the receipt. We'll do it on our way out of town."

"What next?" Jessie asked.

"Sit down and let's talk," Torrey prompted. "First decision—and you may not be ready to make it yet—will you keep the baby?"

"Of course I'll keep it! I may not have wanted to get pregnant, but I would never have an abortion. I couldn't do that to Matt or to any child of his. But I don't want to tell him yet," Jessie said. "I've heard lots of women miscarry in their first three months. I don't think I should get his hopes up."

"Okay, I'll keep your confidence—you know that. But you must see a doctor, an OB/GYN, not old Doc Simmons."

"How do I find a good one? It's not as if I can go around asking new mothers in Spruce Creek."

"The nearest full-service hospital is St. Anthony's South in Lakewood. That's where they took you after your accident with the deer. You can look for an OB/GYN who has privileges there. The hospital will give you a referral."

"I want to do it right now. I don't want to be making any phone calls from the ranch."

"Okay, go for it."

"Torrey, when I make an appointment, will you go with me? I don't want to go alone—at least, not the first time."

"Of course I'll go with you. The two of us going off together will be less suspicious than if you took off for a day by yourself."

"I'm so glad you figured out what was wrong with me. God only knows when I would have. I just never suspected. I'm so dumb."

After getting referrals, Jessie chose one of the doctors recommended by the hospital. She made her choice based on gender. She decided she wanted a woman doctor during her pregnancy, feeling a woman would be more understanding and helpful. She phoned the doctor's office for an appointment. After answering a bunch of questions, Jessie was scheduled for her first prenatal visit in three weeks.

Torrey and Jessie put their heads together, planning their excuse for going to Lakewood. Jessie also had to come up with a good reason for not drinking wine with dinner anymore. That wasn't too difficult to do. She would just claim she was trying to lose weight.

MATT DRIFTED IN AND OUT OF CONSCIOUSNESS. When he was awake he felt cold and damp, and his head hurt badly. He knew he had suffered a concussion and he needed to get to a hospital. But there was no one out here to help him, and he was too weak to do anything for himself. Then before he could form another coherent thought, he would slip back into darkness before rousing again to cold and pain.

He didn't know how long he had been lying in the road when he heard the sound of a vehicle coming up from the highway. Thank God, he thought. *Help was coming.*

Like watching something from a dream, he saw the Range Rover approach and stop, and then Jessie got out of the car. She rushed toward him.

"Matt, Matt!" She sank to her knees beside him. "Oh, Matt."

He groaned. "Wench backlash . . . can't get up."

Jessie jumped up and ran back to the Rover. She came toward him again, this time with blankets that she wrapped around him. She spoke very precisely to him. "Matt, can you understand me?" She leaned close to his ear. "I can't lift you by myself. I'm going to move the truck and go up the road to get help. Do you understand? I'll be right back."

She tucked the blankets tighter around his body and jumped into the ranch truck. She ground the gears but managed to get it straightened out and along the side of the road. She ran back to her Rover and took off driving up the hill at a speed significantly faster than her usual twenty-five miles an hour.

Matt lay still, trusting she would be back as soon as she was able. Jessie wouldn't leave him. He knew she wouldn't.

He drifted in and out of consciousness again, but he was warmer. His head hurt just as badly. That hadn't improved any.

Soon Jessie was back with Tom and Hank. She had a heavy quilt. Tom and Hank rolled the quilt under him. The back seats of her Rover had been flattened out. The two men lifted him gently into the vehicle. Tom got in the passenger seat of the Rover, while Hank hopped into the truck. The two vehicles started down the hill to Guanella Pass Road.

"Matt," Jessie said, "I called for Medevac. The helicopter will land on the pass road and take you to the hospital. I'll follow in the car. Do you understand?"

Matt groaned. He knew he should articulate an answer, but he just couldn't.

He didn't know how long they waited on the side of the road, but eventually he heard the clap-clap sound of rotors and knew the helicopter was coming. The chopper landed well away from the vehicles, but it still stirred up dirt, gravel and dry grass. The pilot powered down the rotors, and then two paramedics jumped out and approached the Rover.

While one took his vitals, the other asked Jessie a bunch of questions. Matt knew she couldn't tell them much since she'd not been there when the accident happened. He tried to talk, but they shushed him. Then they put a plastic collar on his neck and started an IV before they moved him onto a backboard. Tom and Hank got out to help, but the paramedics waved them away. Matt watched as Tom jumped into the truck with Hank. They would return up the hill to the ranch. Jessie would drive to Lakewood and follow him to the hospital.

The door was pulled closed on the helicopter, and the pilot engaged the rotors. Matt felt almost weightless as they lifted up and turned east. He wished he could see the terrain below him. He knew it would be beautiful.

He could hear one of the paramedics talking with an ER doctor on the radio. "White male, six foot three inches tall, approximately two hundred twenty pounds, struck in the back of the head when a wench rope broke and snapped back. Lucky son of a bitch—if that'd been cable instead of rope, he would be dead."

Matt thought if he'd been lucky the rope wouldn't have snapped.

"He apparently lay on a gravel road for a couple of hours until the wife found him and went for help. He is concussed and drifting in an out of consciousness, though he seems to be doing better now that we are getting fluids into him."

"ETA twenty minutes," the pilot called back.

The paramedic repeated the ETA to the doctor and then busied himself with checking Matt's vitals again.

Matt was finally warm enough. He couldn't imagine how he would have survived if it were December instead of August, or if Jessie hadn't found him before dark. When the sun sets at ten thousand feet it gets cold, doesn't matter what month it is.

The helicopter landed on top of the hospital building. Matt's stretcher was lifted out of the chopper and the wheels dropped. He was whisked into a high-speed elevator and launched on a rapid descent into the ER.

A doctor came to examine him immediately. She took all Matt's vitals again. Matt wondered if the doctor didn't trust what the paramedics had just told her, or if she thought Matt's vitals might have changed significantly in a few minutes.

The doctor ordered a blood draw to type and match him in case he required surgery. She ordered an immediate CT scan to check out his skull and brain. Matt could have told her she wouldn't find anything in his head—if he had any brains, he wouldn't have tried harvesting deadfall by himself.

When he heard the sound of Jessie's voice coming into the ER, he knew everything would be all right. Jessie would take care of him—she always did.

ELEVEN

Shaky and breathless, Jessie felt as if she had been in another wreck when she rushed into the ER waiting room. She needed to find Matt. She needed him to be okay. She couldn't be without her husband, especially now.

Grateful it was summer, that all the roads were dry, and that the sun lingered in the sky, Jessie had driven the Rover as fast as she was able. She knew she'd established a personal land speed record for the drive into Lakewood. She was here now, and she wanted to know where they had taken Matt.

She rushed up to an ER clerk. "My husband was brought in by Medevac." Glancing at her watch, she added, "about an hour ago. His name is Matthew Whitaker. Can you tell me where to go to find him?"

The clerk's fingers clicked on a computer keyboard. After a few moments, she was able to tell Jessie that her husband was in an ER treatment room.

"Can I go to him?"

"He's being cared for. But before I let you go in, I need to get some personal information regarding Mr. Whitaker. The paramedics had almost no information for him."

"I brought his wallet with his insurance card. Can we get this done quickly?"

After all the clerk's questions were answered to the best of Jessie's ability, she was allowed into the ER. Hospitals, she thought, should be places of quiet healing. Not so an emergency room. People moved purposefully from place to place, monitors beeped and occasionally screeched. Phones rang and orderlies wheeled gurneys across the floor. Orders were called out.

"I'm Jessica Whitaker. I'm looking for my husband, Matthew Whitaker," she spoke firmly to the first person she encountered.

"Check at the desk," was the answer she received with an arm motion toward a centrally located counter area.

Before Jessie could move in that direction, a

woman approached her. "I am Dr. Malhotra. I'm treating your husband."

"How is he? Can I see him?"

"He has a serious concussion, but no skull fracture. His CT didn't reveal any bleeding into the brain. He must have a very hard head."

"Harder than you can possibly know." Jessie smiled for the first time in hours as the doctor led her to a treatment cubical.

"We will be admitting your husband, Mrs. Whitaker. We'll keep him for at least twenty-four hours. We need to be certain his brain doesn't swell."

The doctor's smile was warm and reassuring. "Go in now," she told Jessie. "Your husband is waiting for you."

Matt reached out a hand to her. "Jess, I'm so glad you're here. I feel better already." He gave her a lopsided grin. "They plan to keep me in the hospital, so I'll suffer another night without you sleeping beside me. I missed you last night."

"Well, if you're worried about sleeping alone, I know you'll recover. Seriously, how do you feel?"

"Like I was hit in the back of the head by a two-by-four. I have a terrible headache. But the doctor won't give me anything stronger than a

Tylenol. She doesn't want me to fall asleep."

Jessie gripped his hand. "Then I'll keep you awake—at least, as long as I'm able." She was very tired and didn't hold out much hope she could stay awake for long.

She left Matt's cubicle long enough to step outside the emergency room and call the ranch. She talked to Tom, assuring him Matt would recover.

When Jessie returned, she asked Matt to tell her how the accident had happened. He told her about his decision to harvest deadfall and bring it up to be cut for firewood. He didn't remember much after moving the rock that had hung up the line—only searing pain and fading in and out of consciousness, and the despair he would die without seeing Jessie again.

She shared with him a few of the things she and Torrey had done while at The Broadmoor. She almost felt guilty not sharing everything. But especially now, he didn't need any more excitement.

When the orderly came to take Matt up to a patient room, Jessie was allowed to walk along with him. His clothes had been placed, mud and all, into a heavy-duty plastic bag that had his name written across the front. The bag was set on top of his feet and he was wheeled away.

She walked along beside Matt. The orderly made a point of telling her when he was going to stop or turn or enter the elevator. Jessie appreciated his thoughtfulness. It meant she could keep pace and not be surprised.

When they reached the patient floor, the orderly checked in with a nurse. He then asked Jessie to remain in the hallway until he had Matt settled into his bed. They disappeared behind a closed door. Before long the orderly exited the room, pushing the now-empty gurney, and told her she could go in.

Jessie was pleased to see Matt was in a private room. It had all the necessary medical paraphernalia built into the wall at the head of Matt's bed. His window looked out toward the foothills. Jessie could see the sun sinking to the west as dusk advanced. Instead of the inevitable hard plastic visitor's chair, there was a comfortable looking recliner in the corner. She was grateful because she intended to spend the night if the hospital would allow it.

A nurse bustled into the room, identified herself as Ellen, and immediately took Matt's vitals. Then she poured fresh water into a plastic cup from the standard plastic hospital pitcher and handed it to him. Jessie knew they would be pushing fluids even though Matt was hooked up to an IV. Ellen showed Matt how to operate his bed and told him to ring if he needed anything. She promised to return with some supper for Matt and asked Jessie if she would like a tray as well.

Matt looked at Jessie and said, "I don't know if she is promising dinner, or threatening."

MATT WANTED TO GO HOME SO HE COULD GET some rest. Every time he dozed off it seemed as if someone came into his hospital room and woke him up.

Jessie agreed. She would be happy when they could leave.

The nurse had allowed her to stay. Jessie claimed the chair had been comfortable enough, but every hour Matt was awakened and, while not intentional, she was too. So Matt knew Jessie was as tired as he.

When the meal service employee delivered Matt's breakfast, she asked if Jessie would like a tray, but Jessie declined. She told Matt she wanted to wash up, get some real coffee with caffeine in it, and have some onions and peppers in her eggs.

He laughed at her and expressed the wish he could join her.

After Jessie left, Matt risked getting out of bed to use the patient bathroom. He was a little shaky, but overall he didn't feel too badly. He still had a headache, but his head no longer felt as if it might explode. He would mend.

It had been tricky disconnecting the IV bag from the ram's horn holder next to the bed, but he managed and carried it with him. But he didn't want to drag the stand with him into the bathroom. He'd disconnected the plastic clothespin-type apparatus that was on his finger. Apparently, that had set off some sort of alarm at the nurses' station because before he knew it a nurse was knocking on the bathroom door.

"Mr. Whitaker, are you all right?"

"I'm fine. I'm just enjoying my morning meditation."

"You should not have tried to go to the bathroom alone. There should be someone with you."

"I've been going to the bathroom alone since I was three years old. Leave me in peace, and I will be out when I'm ready."

After washing his hands, Matt examined his

head in the bathroom mirror. His skull had been shaved so the gash in his scalp could be stitched and bandaged. He decided when he got home, he would have the rest of his hair cut short so he didn't look too strange when his hair began to grow back. He had a few other bruises, but nothing serious. In fact, for someone who had come as close to dying as he had, he looked damn good.

"Mr. Whitaker?"

The nurse was back. *No point in fighting city hall.*

"I'm coming out. I'm fine."

The nurse had straightened his bed while he'd been in the bathroom. He handed her the IV bottle and she put it back on the ram's horn with a look of disapproval. When he was settled back under the covers, the nurse put the clothespin back on his finger.

"What's that thing called?" he asked her.

"It's a pulse oximeter. When you disconnected it from your finger, the monitor signaled you had no oxygen in your blood."

"That wouldn't be good."

She frowned. "No, it wouldn't. That's why we came running."

"I'm bored. Can I walk around?"

"If you'll behave for the next thirty or forty minutes, I'll get you a portable IV stand, get slippers on your feet, and another hospital gown to cover your back side, and then we'll let you walk up and down the corridor. But I have other patients to take care of first."

He realized he was making life difficult for a nurse who was doing nothing more than trying to take care of him and help him get well. So, he settled back and decided to turn on the TV. After running through the available channels, he decided turning the TV on was a huge mistake, and turned it off again.

He wished Jessie would return. He could entertain himself just looking at her. He knew she had no idea how beautiful she was.

After what seemed like three hours the nurse returned. While she had been gone, some maintenance-type person had pushed a wheeled IV stand into Matt's room. The nurse made short work of transferring the IV bottle to the ram's horn on the mobile stand. Then she handed Matt some sock-type slippers for him to put on his feet. Finally, she took a hospital gown and draped it around the back of him, unfastening and refastening snaps on the shoulder that allowed him to wear his IV without a problem.

Matt grinned, "I'm impressed. You have all kinds of gadgets and gizmos to make things work—gowns that don't require putting your arm through a sleeve, clothespins that measure oxygen, IV stands on wheels, one-size-fits-all slippers. Who thinks up all this stuff?"

"Mr. Whitaker," the nurse said with a laugh, "I'm assuming you've never stayed in a hospital before."

"No, ma'am. Only time I've been in a hospital is when my wife was in the emergency room after she had an encounter with a deer on a dark highway. We only stayed long enough for the doctors to check her out and tell her she was fit to go home."

"Well, sir, there is a whole industry devoted to creating equipment designed to make a patient's stay in the hospital as healing as possible and, at the same time, keeping the patient comfortable."

Matt walked the corridors on his patient floor until Jessie returned. Then he returned to his room so he could be with her.

"What do you have in the packages?" he asked when he settled back into his bed.

"I didn't think you would want to wear your muddy clothes home. So I went to Macy's and bought you underwear, some new Levi's, and a long sleeved T-shirt."

Before Matt could tell Jessie that she was the best wife in the world, Dr. Malhotra came into the room. "I'm sending you down for another CT. If it is clear, you can go home."

Matt and Jessie grinned at each other.

"But you will take it easy for a week after you get home, and your wife must drive. I don't want you endangering the rest of the population by getting behind the wheel of a car until you're completely healed."

Turning to look at Jessie, Dr. Malhotra said, "If his headaches get worse, or if he experiences any dizziness or blurry vision, bring him back into the ER immediately."

WHEN JESSIE TURNED ONTO THE RANCH ROAD, she saw Matt looking out the windows at the side of the track, apparently trying to spot exactly where his accident had happened. But she didn't see any deadfall anywhere along their route. Then it occurred to her that the hands had harvested all the downed timber so Matt wouldn't have any excuse to repeat his folly.

"Looks like Tom and the men have cleared all the debris, probably have it all chopped and stacked, as well. Good thing if they do, because you cannot chop wood nor do anything else strenuous until you are completely healed."

"Is making love with my wife strenuous?"

"Probably not—as long as you are lying down."

"I can agree to that."

They continued the word play the rest of the way up to the house. When they pulled into the drive, all the hands had gathered around to welcome Matt home. They greeted him and expressed happiness he was not seriously injured. They insisted he was not to do any heavy work, and pointed out that was why he had employed them.

Consuela came out on the porch and down the stairs. "*Señor* Matt, we have been so worried. It is good you are home. I will fix you a good dinner—better than the food they give you in the hospital."

Jessie watched Matt hug the housekeeper. She was so grateful for Consuela. It occurred to Jessie that taking care of a new baby wouldn't be too difficult because Consuela would be here to cook and clean. Jessie had very little help when

Jordan and Jeremy were small. Having a child of her own wouldn't be the same at all as raising her brothers.

When Matt was settled in a comfortable chair in the great room, Tom came in to talk about ranch business with him. Jessie stayed nearby to be certain nothing Tom had to say would rile Matt and get him upset. She served both men iced tea and some of Consuela's homemade cookies.

When it appeared the conversation would be banal, she went into the laundry room and dumped the bag with Matt's clothing. She was happy to find the quilt she had wrapped him in had found its way home. It was filthy, but it would wash, as would Matt's dirty Levi's and shirt.

As she held the quilt in her hands, she began to shake. She relived the horror of finding her husband unconscious and injured. If she believed in signs and omens, she would think she had received a cosmic warning. If she didn't value what she had with Matt, she could easily lose him.

She wasn't ready to say she was happy to be pregnant, but she was prepared to give the idea time to grow on her. She knew Matt would be ecstatic when she told him—but not yet. She guessed she was probably four or five weeks along. By the time she saw the OB /GYN she would be seven or eight weeks. If the doctor didn't see any signs of risk, maybe she would tell Matt after her first prenatal visit—or maybe not.

Jessie was startled out of her reverie by the sound of the ringing phone. When she answered it, her brother Jordan started talking in an accusatory voice. "Where have you been? I've been trying to reach you. Kat went into labor and gave birth to our daughter, Faith Marie, at 8:41 this morning. When I got no answer at the house except voice mail, I tried calling your iPhone."

"Jordan, stop," Jessie broke in on her brother's excited account. "No one was here to answer the phone because Matt was injured yesterday. He was in the hospital, and I stayed with him so my phone was turned off."

"What happened? Is he okay?" Jordan abruptly changed the direction of his comments.

"He was clearing deadwood, the wench rope snapped, and he was caught in the backlash. He was airlifted to St. Anthony in Lakewood, and kept overnight for observation. I just brought him home. He'll recover, but he's going to have a nasty headache for a while." Jessie sighed. "What about Kat and the baby? Are they okay?"

"Mother and child are doing great. We must have all been at the hospital at the same time. Under the circumstances, I guess I can forgive you for not answering my call." Jessie could hear teasing in her brother's voice.

They chatted on the phone for thirty minutes, exchanging the details of their exciting news. Jessie was happy to hear Kat had an easy time of it. For a first baby, Faith had come quickly, according to Jordan.

When she finally got off the phone, Jessie went to find her husband to share the news of the new addition to the family. When they went into dinner, they found Consuela had outdone herself. She prepared grilled *carne asada* and homemade flour tortillas. On the side she served Baja black beans, corn and rice. Dessert was *sopapillas* dusted in powdered sugar and filled with honey. Jessie ate more than she should and knew she would suffer for it later.

Fortunately, Matt was supposed to stay away from alcohol for at least a week. So Jessie didn't need to come up with an excuse for not having a beer with dinner. They both drank iced tea.

"What did Tom want to talk about?" Jessie asked as they lingered over their dessert.

"He's seeing indications of trespassers up

above the tree line. It appears the signs posted down on the highway are working, but he thinks some people may have hiked in from Mt. Bierstadt."

"Are they damaging the fences or leaving rubbish behind?"

"No. But it does appear he, or they, may have built a campfire. As dry as the grasses and the forests are this time of year, any fire is a risk. And a fire built by a fool, who doesn't realize he shouldn't be building a fire at all, isn't likely to be the safest fire around."

"What are you going to do?"

"I think I should take Tom and cold camp up on the ridge for a night or two. We would be able to see anybody who intrudes."

"No! Absolutely not! You are recovering from a serious concussion. You aren't going to be out of my sight for at least a week."

"But, Jess, this person could be dangerous. Remember those yahoos who were looking for a pot farm? This could be motivated by something similar."

"All the more reason you aren't going to play at being a detective on a stake-out. Call the sheriff, let him investigate. Call the State Forestry Service—they're charged with preventing wild fires, or call the State Patrol. Tom and a couple of the hands can cold camp, but you are not going to."

"I don't like to ask my employees to do something I can't, or won't, do myself. And this is important, Jess."

"Am I important to you, Matt?"

"You know you are. You are the most important person in my life."

"Then don't, for the second time in a week, risk making me a widow. When I saw you lying there on the road, I almost stopped breathing."

"Good thing you didn't. Your quick thinking and decisive action saved my life."

"Then trust my judgment. Let others investigate and resolve this problem."

Jessie did her best to give Matt a 'come hither' look. "Let's go to bed early. You can see if my judgment is trustworthy or not."

TWELVE

WEEKS HAD PASSED SINCE MATT'S ACCIDENT. Labor Day had come and gone. The headaches had diminished, his hair was growing back, and Matt felt damn lucky to be alive. Jessie was being especially affectionate. Matt felt guilty he had put her through such a stressful incident, but he was not going to complain about her attentions. He enjoyed every minute, even if she was acting like a drill sergeant when she thought he might be overdoing it.

The Park County Sheriff had come out to the ranch and ridden with Matt up to the area that Tom said showed sign of trespassers. The sheriff agreed it appeared someone had built a small campfire. And while there was no fire circle enclosed in rocks, the area had been scraped clear of grasses. So apparently the person wasn't a complete ignoramus. The sheriff would share his findings with the State Patrol and they would keep a sharp lookout. But unless they stationed someone in the area, it would be almost impossible to catch anyone.

Matt was in his office at his computer doing some research. He'd been fascinated by the equipment he'd come in contact with while in the hospital. Surfing the Internet, looking at medical equipment manufacturers and their products, he acknowledged he might need to diversify his holdings. Everything in his vast financial empire was associated with agribusiness or construction. People were not going to stop getting sick and injured any more than they would stop eating. He would have his business manager look into the possibility of expanding his investments.

The phone rang. He answered it without looking at caller ID. "Whitaker."

A female voice asked, "Is Mrs. Whitaker available?"

"I'm sorry, she's not here right now. May I take a message?" Matt knew Jessie had driven down to Spruce Creek to visit with Torrey.

"This is Dr. Graham's nurse at Lakewood OB/GYN. I'm just calling to remind her of her appointment tomorrow afternoon."

Matt hesitated for a second. Jessie hadn't said anything about a doctor's appointment. "Okay, I'll make certain she gets the message."

The nurse thanked him and ended the call.

Matt went back to surfing the Internet, but the phone call was very much at the forefront of his mind. Jessie hadn't mentioned having an appointment in Lakewood with a gynecologist. Was she having female problems she didn't want to talk about? And why go all that way to see a doctor? Why not make an appointment with Doc Simmons, or one of the young Turks—Scott Petersen or Mike Larsen?

In his mind, Matt wrestled with imaginary illnesses. *Cancer! Did Jess have ovarian cancer?* No, that didn't make sense; she would be seeing an oncologist, not a gynecologist. He had worked himself into a state of near madness when he finally heard Jessie's Rover pulling up in front of the house.

He didn't want to make a big scene, so he wandered out to the great room as Jessie was coming through the front door. He did his best to appear casual.

"Hi, honey, did you and Torrey have a good visit?" he asked as he wrapped her in a big hug.

"We did. She's like a mother to me, so easy to talk to."

Matt's brain whirled—*easy to talk to*—Jessie needed someone who was easy to talk to.

"Oh, by the way, I took a message for you. Dr. Graham's office called."

Matt watched Jessie's face. No comprehension.

"Lakewood OB/GYN phoned to remind you about your appointment tomorrow."

Now Matt saw the color leave Jessie's face entirely. She went as white as fresh-fallen snow.

"Why didn't you tell me you had made an appointment to see a gynecologist?" he asked gently. He didn't want to sound accusatory.

"I completely forgot. I made the appointment the day you were injured. It slipped my mind with everything else that happened."

His voice changed now. "You were in Colorado Springs that day. Are you telling me, that while you were on a spa vacation at The Broadmoor Resort, you phoned a doctor in Lakewood and made an appointment?"

"Matt, this sounds like an inquisition. What are you getting at?"

"Jessie, I'm worried about you. Are you sick? What aren't you telling me?"

"Oh, sweetheart, I'm not sick. Torrey and I were having a girls-only outing. We started talking about female things when I realized it was time for me to see a gynecologist. Torrey being Torrey insisted I make an appointment immediately before I forgot."

"Why not see Doc Simmons or one of the young Turks?" Matt asked.

"I don't want to see Doc Simmons because he's getting old and he's only a GP. As for Doctors Petersen and Larsen, they are primarily urgent care. Most importantly, for female issues, I want a woman doctor."

Matt thought about what Jessie was telling him. Everything she said made sense in a way. *But why had the color left her face when he told her it was the gynecologist's office?* That made no sense at all.

He didn't think Jessie was lying to him, but he suspected she wasn't telling him the entire story. There was more to be uncovered.

"Would you like me to drive you into town tomorrow when you go for your appointment? I don't like you making that long drive by yourself."

"Torrey is going with me. We're going to go shopping at Belmar and have lunch at the Baker Street Pub. I've been craving shepherd's pie, and while Consuela is the best Mexican food cook west of the Mississippi, she doesn't do British too well."

"You're spending a lot of time with Torrey," Matt said. "I guess I'm jealous of the stuff you two are enjoying together."

"Oh, Matt, don't be. While I was busy being a mother to my brothers, Torrey was the nearest thing to a mother I had. I've just rediscovered how important she is to me."

"I know, Jess. I'm being selfish, I guess. I want you with me all the time."

"You had my undivided attention for an entire week. I thought you'd like the opportunity to escape my supervision." Jessie gave him a sweet smile and Matt dropped the subject. He would pursue this later.

JESSIE FLED THE GREAT ROOM. SHE FOUND keeping secrets from her husband was a tricky business, and not easily done. *But who would have expected him to intercept a phone call from the obstetrician's office?*

She realized now she would have to tell Matt about the baby immediately after the doctor's visit. She would have prenatal vitamins to take and she wouldn't be able to drink wine or beer. He would notice. Fortunately, she had never smoked so that wasn't an issue. And then there was the question of riding. How long before she was denied the pleasure of mounting a horse and wandering off to the High Country? She accepted that even before the child arrived, her life would change drastically.

What would her brothers think? Would they be happy at the prospect of becoming uncles? They would assume she and Matt would be staying together. Jordan and Jeremy both knew the two of them had issues, but she made certain they never knew what and why. She didn't want them to feel any guilt at stealing her childhood. It wasn't their fault. It was the fault of the mother who'd abandoned them.

In her own mind she made the same assumption. There would be no divorce now. She trembled, overwhelmed. There were so many *what ifs* to consider.

All day, Jessie did her best to avoid being alone with Matt when he might want to talk. When they fell into bed at night she immediately pursued seducing him so he had no time to think of asking questions. It wasn't a hardship. She loved her husband and what they shared. So that night she kept him distracted the best way she knew how.

On Wednesday morning, she left the ranch before nine o'clock. She drove down to Spruce Creek, picked Torrey up at home, and began the drive northeast to Lakewood. She confessed her near miss with Matt because of the intercepted phone call.

"I know I must tell him about the pregnancy after this visit to the doctor. It'll be impossible to keep my condition a secret any longer."

"Why would you want to?" Torrey asked.

"Because once I tell Matt, this will all be real."

"Jess, it's all very real right now. This isn't a dream or a fantasy. You *are* going to be a mother in eight months more or less. Telling Matt will let you get used to the idea."

"I guess you're right."

They drove on in silence. They did shop at the Belmar. Jessie bought a layette and some other baby things that she asked Torrey to keep for her until after Matt knew what was happening. She ate her shepherd's pie at Baker Street, but she was so distraught, she barely tasted it.

When they arrived at the obstetrician's office, it was almost anticlimactic. She was handed a sheaf of papers to fill out. Some of the questions she was unable to answer, like whether her mother was still living or deceased. Other questions were to be expected, like whether this was her first pregnancy. And when was her last period? Jessie answered everything to the best of her ability.

Before long the doctor came in, introduced herself as Dr. Graham, and encouraged Jessie to relax. She went over Jessie's medical history.

"Why don't you know if your mother is still living?" the doctor asked.

"Because she abandoned the family when I was ten years old. No one has heard from her since."

"Does her abandonment cause you any hesitancy about your own pregnancy?"

"It does," Jessie answered honestly. "I intended never to get pregnant."

"How does your husband feel about the pregnancy?"

"He doesn't know," Jessie confessed. "But once you confirm I'm indeed pregnant, I plan to tell him."

The doctor continued asking questions, and

then had Jessie lay back on the exam table.

When she finished with her exam she said, "I estimate you are eight or nine weeks pregnant which gives you a due date around March twenty-seventh. Everything appears to be normal."

Dr. Graham helped Jessie sit up. "I do have one concern, however. You live at an altitude of roughly ten thousand feet, is that correct?"

"Ninety-seven hundred, give or take fifty feet. Why is that a concern?"

"Babies born at high altitude tend to have smaller birth weights. And there can be—I'm not saying there will be—but there can be an increased risk of premature birth," Dr. Graham replied.

"What should I do? I can't move to a lower altitude for seven or eight months."

"While it would be desirable, I'm not going to ask you to do that. But I am going to insist you not go higher than the level at which you live. Secondly, I don't want you doing anything the least bit rigorous. I assume since you live on a ranch you have horses."

"Yes," Jessie answered.

"No horseback riding. No heavy lifting. You must treat your pregnancy as if it is high risk because at that altitude it is, even if you have no other physical issues we're aware of."

"Okay . . ."

"And six full weeks before your delivery date, I want you to move close to Lakewood and the hospital, let's say by Valentine's Day. I know of some families that take in unwed mothers, and while that isn't true in your case, they'll provide you with a room and a loving environment."

"That won't be necessary, Doctor. My husband can afford to rent a house for us."

Dr. Graham wrote prescriptions for prenatal vitamins and iron pills. She instructed Jessie to eat a well-balanced diet and do some easy exercise every day, preferably walking on a level surface for twenty or thirty minutes.

"I want to see you in four weeks," Dr. Graham instructed, "and bring your husband with you."

WHEN THEY LEFT DR. GRAHAM'S OFFICE, JESSIE and Torrey stopped at the pharmacy in the medical office building to fill the prescriptions Jessie had been given. She had received a written summary of her doctor's visit. She had specific instructions about diet and exercise, and she had handouts about pregnancy and preparing for childbirth—one pamphlet for her and a different one for Matt.

After the two women were on the road toward home, Jessie said, "You won't need to hide the purchases I made today, Torrey. I might as well take the baby clothes with me. That may be the easiest way to tell Matt I'm expecting."

"Are you trying to be subtle?" Torrey asked.

"No, just the opposite. I'll show him what I bought today, and he'll realize I'm pregnant."

"I wouldn't count on it, Jess. Men are obtuse at times. They totally misunderstand things we think are obvious."

"We'll see," Jessie said, convinced her bright and intelligent husband would reach the correct conclusion immediately.

When they arrived in Spruce Creek, Jessie dropped Torrey off at home. It was late in the day and there was no point taking her to the clinic. "Call me this evening and let me know what happens," Torrey requested.

"Okay," Jessie responded before she drove off.

When she finally reached the ranch house, the sun was far in the west but it was still daylight. Matt should be around somewhere.

She called out to her husband as she came into the great room.

Consuela answered her. "*Señor* Matt rode off with the sheriff right after lunch, *Señora*. He did not say when he would be back."

"Did they go on horseback or in a vehicle?" Jessie asked.

"They took the horses, *Señora*."

"Thank you, Consuela. I'll go find Tom and see what he can tell me."

Jessie took her purchases into her bedroom and changed from her 'go to the city' clothes to her everyday 'work around the ranch' clothing. She was more than a little irritated with her husband. When she wanted him to be at home asking her questions, he was up on the mountain doing God knows what.

Keeping in mind what the doctor had told her about exceeding the altitude at which the ranch house sat, she went no further than the first barn which was on the same level as the house. When she didn't find Matt's foreman or any other ranch hands at the barn, she considered ringing the big bell on the porch of the house. But the bell was only for signaling a crisis. And no matter how urgently she wanted to know where her husband was and when he would be back, she admitted her need to know wasn't truly an emergency.

So Jessie returned to the house, poured herself a glass of vegetable juice, and settled into a porch chair to await her husband's return. The doctor had cautioned her to stay hydrated. So the juice accomplished two goals, hydration and nutrition. Jessie was feeling very proud of herself.

Just as the sun was preparing to sink behind the Continental Divide, she saw Matt and the sheriff ride their horses down to the barn. A couple of hands followed them on foot from the upper barn, obviously planning to remove the horses' tack, brush them down, and settle them for the night.

When they left the lower barn, the sheriff climbed into his truck and started down past the house on his way to the highway. He tooted the horn and gave Jessie a friendly wave as he drove by. Matt wandered down toward the house on foot. He was obviously tired and very dirty.

He gave Jessie a hug and told her he needed to shower and shave before he did anything else. Jessie followed him into the bedroom.

"Go shower," she said. "I have something to show you when you're done."

"What are you going to show me? Did you

get me a present?" Matt asked.

"I'll show you when you get out of the shower. Now go."

While Matt was in the shower, Jessie took the layette and the baby clothes out of the shopping bag and laid them out on the bed. She had purchased greens and yellows since it was too early to have any guess as to the gender. She was excited while she waited for Matt to finish cleaning up. *What's taking him so long?*

He came out into the bedroom with a towel wrapped about his waist. Droplets of water were sprinkled across his body—a spear of dark hair arrowed down his chest and belly. Jessie was overpowered with love and desire.

"So, what did you want to show me?" Matt asked, completely oblivious to her reaction.

Taking a deep breath, Jessie gestured to the clothes on the bed. "See what I bought today?"

"Nice, who do we know having a baby?"

Jessie wanted to scream in frustration. Torrey had been right. Matt was being completely obtuse.

"Matt, I went to see the OB/GYN today. I was seeing her for her specialty in obstetrics, not gynecology."

Jessie watched Matt's face as the realization

he was going to become a father dawned on him.

"We're pregnant? We're going to have a baby?" Matt embraced her and covered her face with kisses. Then he stopped and set her away from him. "How do you feel about it?"

"I'm not certain yet. But I'm not going to do anything to stop it. I will have our child and I will do my best to be a good mother."

Matt hugged her again. "You'll be a wonderful mother—the best. I know."

"I'll try. I will do my very best."

"How long have you known?" he asked.

"I've suspected since the day of your accident. Obviously, that was not the time to tell you. As for knowing, I didn't know for sure until today."

THIRTEEN

When Matt awoke the next morning, he was walking on air. He was going to be a father, but when? He hadn't asked Jessie the due date.

He couldn't contain himself. He wanted to tell the world. He and Jessie discussed who they should tell immediately and who could find out through the Park County grapevine.

They would tell Jessie's brothers. Torrey, of course, already knew but had promised to let Jessie and Matt announce the blessed event to Jordan and Jeremy. At the ranch they would tell Consuela and Tom—both needed to know for Jessie's protection when Matt was away. In his own mind, Matt had no intention of being away with any degree of frequency, and certainly not for any length of time.

Once again, Matt was grateful for the improvements he had made to secure power and communications at the ranch.

Jessie had cautioned him. She'd explained about the added risk of high altitude. She'd given him all the papers and pamphlets from the doctor so he would know everything she knew. The first one he wanted to read was *The Importance of You, the Father, during Pregnancy.*

Matt thought it was nice someone recognized fathers were important beyond being sperm donors. The pamphlet stressed the need for the father to be involved in the mother's pregnancy, to be supportive, to be patient and understanding, to take an interest in whatever plans the mother-to-be wished to make. The pamphlet discussed the hormonal changes Jessie would undergo. It explained cravings. It encouraged a continuing loving relationship so the mother-to-be wouldn't feel ugly, or fat, or unattractive. Matt was relieved to learn he and Jessie could continue to have sexual relations for as long as she wanted. Knowing his passionate bride, he didn't think she would be kicking him out of bed any time soon.

Enlightenment suddenly struck. The major issue in his marriage had been resolved. The decision to have children—which he'd left up to

Jessie—had been made. Perhaps not by deliberate choice, but subconsciously Jessie had allowed it to happen. The likelihood of divorce had moved far from the table. He knew he couldn't backslide. He couldn't take Jessie for granted. But fate had intervened to strengthen his marriage.

He went to the kitchen for a cup of coffee and then to his office to start making lists.

First they should decide on which room to make into a nursery. He thought the bedroom directly across the hall from their room would be best, but he would ask Jessie what she thought before he offered any suggestions. He would need to paint it. They would buy baby furniture. Jessie had already started buying baby clothes. Thinking about how she used the baby clothes to let him know they were expecting was cute.

The baby would need a nurse just as soon as he came home from the hospital. One of Jessie's concerns had been mothering another child after raising her brothers. Matt wanted to be certain Jessie could continue her career. He knew she would be a loving mother, but he didn't want her to be burdened with any of the more unpleasant chores of child rearing. He only wanted her to enjoy the good times.

Matt was looking forward to teaching his son

to fish and hunt—after he was older, of course—to love the land that would one day belong to the child, his heir. Even though Jessie said it was too soon to know the child's gender, Matt was certain he had fathered a boy. But if he was wrong, he would teach his daughter to fish and to hunt. Nothing said girls couldn't learn those skills, as well.

His mind bounced back to his contemplation of the nursery. They should decorate it with a western theme: cowboys, cattle trains, campfires, chuck wagons, mountains, and prairies. He was so deep into his contemplation that he was startled when Jessie came into his office.

"Hi, you look deep in thought. What are you dreaming about?"

"Decorating our son's nursery."

"Whoa, there, cowboy. We may just as easily have a girl. Then what?"

"I'll dream about decorating our daughter's nursery," he said.

Matt reached around and pulled Jessie into his lap. He rested his hand on her stomach, "Our child is resting here. I can't describe my feelings. I am awestruck." As his hand was slipping upwards under her sweater, his phone rang. Matt groaned as he reached to answer it, tightening his hold on his wife. "Don't go away."

"Whitaker," he barked into the handset.

"Mr. Whitaker, this is Detective Turner at the Park County Sheriff's Department."

"Yes, detective, what can I do for you?"

"It's more what I can do for you, Mr. Whitaker. Rangers found a car parked about a mile up the highway from your access road. When they checked the area, they discovered the fence was cut and assumed someone had intruded onto your property. They called us for backup and then started tracking. When we caught up with them, they had a man in custody who claims he knows you and has permission to be on your property. Does the name Bart Ayers mean anything to you?"

There was a long pause and then Matt asked Jessie, "Was Bart Ayers the name of that smarmy photographer that was here for Jordan's birthday barbecue?"

"Yes, I think so. Why?"

Speaking into the phone once again, Matt said, "Turner, Ayers was here on the ranch in the middle of May. Claimed he was interested in photographing Mt. Bierstadt from my property. I think I told him I would consider it, but we never heard from him again. He certainly did not have permission to cut my fence, nor to come onto my property without specific consent."

"Okay, we will hold him over for misdemeanor trespass and property destruction. You'll be required to sign a complaint within the next twenty-four hours either at the substation in Bailey or the sheriff's office in Fairplay."

When he concluded the call Jessie asked, "What was that all about?"

"Rangers caught a trespasser on ranch property. Sheriff has him in custody. I need to go sign a complaint. Want to come along?"

"Where do we have to go?"

"Bailey or Fairplay? You get to choose."

"Bailey's closer and we don't need to cross Kenosha Pass . . . altitude, remember? We'll get back to the ranch sooner. I don't want to miss whatever Consuela is fixing for lunch."

"We could eat out if you like."

"You're kidding, right? There isn't a restaurant in either place that serves food as good as Consuela's.

"Bailey it is."

AS JESSIE FASTENED HER SEAT BELT, SHE WAS pleased she did not need to let it out. She wondered when she would begin to show. She would ask the doctor when she saw her next in October.

She had mixed feelings about the changes her body would undergo. She was already experiencing some mild stomach upset when she first got up in the morning, but she wasn't suffering from what she had been given to believe was morning sickness. She could tolerate herbal tea and dry wheat toast. That was fine with her, because she didn't think caffeine was especially good for an unborn baby. Maybe that was the purpose of morning sickness, to discourage expectant mothers from eating and drinking things that wouldn't be good for the fetus.

She tired easily, but she had been told that was normal. Since she was supposed to get plenty of rest and avoid extreme exertion, maybe this symptom was also for the benefit of her unborn child.

She wasn't convinced her moodiness was to anyone's benefit. She knew it was the result of hormonal changes, but she didn't like it. And she hoped it would pass quickly. She was afraid, however, it wouldn't. She just prayed Matt would be patient with her.

Will he still love me and find me attractive when I balloon to the size and shape of the Goodyear blimp? She prayed he would. He was the one, after all was said and done, who wanted this baby. It wasn't as if she would do anything to end the pregnancy, but she would be happier had it never happened. Her eyes filled with tears as she felt sorry for herself.

"Jess, what's wrong? You have tears in your eyes. Are you hurting? Have I said something to upset you?" Matt leaned over the console to embrace her.

"Matt, nothing is wrong other than I'm being a silly pregnant lady. I was just worrying that you won't love me when I'm huge and ugly."

"Oh, sweetheart, I will always love you. It won't matter how you look or how large you become. I love you, Jessie, the person who resides inside your skin and bones. It's wonderful you're so beautiful, but I would love you even if you weren't."

That was all it took to release the spigots. Jessie started sobbing aloud, tears streaming down her face.

"Jess, Jess, it's okay, honey. Please don't be sad."

"Silly man," Jessie sobbed in reply. "I'm not sad. I'm happy—happy you love me no matter what. These are tears of joy."

Matt looked at his wife in mild exasperation. "How am I supposed to know the difference?"

Jessie started to hiccup. "You're not," she said between convulsive gasps for air. She held her breath in an effort to stop the spasms. Ultimately, she was successful, but not until multiple gulps had escaped.

Matt started the Rover and began the drive down the ranch road. Jessie asked him to stop in Spruce Creek so she could tell Jordan about the impending birth of his niece or nephew. When they arrived behind the clinic, Jessie jumped out of the SUV and rushed through the 'employees only' door. As luck would have it, no one was in sight.

She rushed toward the front with Matt following on her heels. She spotted Torrey and called out to her. The two women embraced as if they hadn't seen each other in decades instead of less than twenty-four hours.

Jordan walked out of his office, followed by Kat. "Sis, what's going on? Torrey's been as itchy as a kid with poison oak."

Jessie couldn't restrain herself. "Jordan,

you're going to be an uncle!"

Her brother stood speechless for a minute, and then he embraced his brother-in-law in a man hug. "Congratulations, Bro! That's wonderful."

"Why are you congratulating him? I'm the one who's pregnant. I'm going to have the baby, not him."

Jordan embraced her. "I wasn't certain you'd want to be congratulated, Sis. I didn't think you wanted another family."

"Oh." Jessie was touched by Jordan's sensitivity. "It's true—I didn't choose to get pregnant. But now that it's happened, I'm content."

Kat hugged her next. "Wonderful. Faith is going to have a cousin. When is the baby due?" she inquired.

"March twenty-seventh, and because of the risk associated with high altitude pregnancies at my age, I'll be moving to Lakewood by Valentine's Day."

"If there's anything we can do, be certain to call us," Kat said. "Torrey or I can be there in thirty minutes provided the road isn't closed by snow. You know we'll come right away. Jordan, too, if you need him."

Jessie felt overwhelmed with her family's love

as she was embraced in a group hug—Torrey, the foster mother who had stepped into the breach when her natural mother had abandoned them; Jordan, the older of her two brothers who had tried to shoulder the responsibilities as man of the house when their dad surrendered that authority; Kat, the sister she had always wished for; and Matt, her husband, the rock, constant and unmovable, to whom she could always cling.

"So the rumors are true."

The group sprung apart as if they'd been caught engaged in a conspiracy.

"What rumors, Jeremy?" Jessie asked her sibling, who had unexpectedly barged into the clinic.

"Why, that you're going to be a mother, of course."

"How could you possibly know that? My doctor only confirmed it yesterday."

"Sis, I keep telling you and Jordan that I have sources in all kinds of places. I can't disclose who they are, of course, but they're usually accurate."

"Jeremy Walker, you tell me right now who told you I'm pregnant."

"No can do, but congratulations to you and Matt. I know you'll be a wonderful mother to my niece or nephew, just as you were to me." Jeremy stepped in to claim a hug and kissed Jessie on the cheek. "Your child will be very lucky to have you as a mom."

"I HATE TO BREAK UP THIS FAMILY REUNION," Matt said, "but we need to get to the sheriff's substation in Bailey to file a complaint."

That was the wrong thing to say, because now Matt had to explain the reasons for filing a complaint, which further delayed their departure. But it did give him an opportunity to ask if any of them had noticed the weird photographer at the birthday barbecue more than three months earlier.

Jeremy admitted to remembering Ayers because Matt had sent him up to stay with Jessie while she was with Ayers. "Strange guy," Jeremy remarked. "Very interested in what I did for a living."

"What did you tell him?" Matt asked.

"Don't you remember? I told him I was a troubleshooter—that I made problems of the two-legged sort go away."

Matt laughed. "I do remember. Seems to me Ayers went away right after that. Why don't you come to Bailey with me? You can share your valuable observations with the deputies."

"I'm not certain how anxious they'll be to listen to my observations. They weren't real happy with me when I interfered regarding the break-in here at the clinic last year."

"I seem to remember something about that. Didn't you go head-to-head with the detective in charge of the case?"

"Yeah, name of Turner. For the longest time, he was convinced Jordan was the bad guy."

Matt chose not to say anything more, but grabbed Jessie's hand to lead her out of the clinic. Jeremy followed them and hopped into the back seat of the Rover.

The end of summer was fast approaching. Traffic was far lighter on Highway 285 than during the tourist season, so the short drive to the Bailey substation took less than thirty minutes. Matt's mind was on his baby-to-be as he listened to the banter between his wife and his brother-in-law.

Jessie wanted to know how Jeremy had known she was pregnant. Jeremy continued to stonewall, and his sister just became more and more frustrated. Matt was glad to arrive at the sheriff's office because he was afraid Jessie was about to explode, she was so annoyed.

The deputy on duty, a grizzled veteran by the name of Harps, took them into an interview room. He asked a series of questions. What did they know about Ayers? Who had brought him to the barbecue? What kind of behavior had he exhibited?

Matt had questions of his own. Where on his property had Ayers been found? What was he doing? Did he even have a camera with him?

The four of them spent about forty minutes exhausting the subject of Bart Ayers. When they were finished, the deputy typed up a complaint form for Matt to sign.

On the way back to Spruce Creek, Matt invited Jeremy to join them for lunch. "I can drop you at your truck, and you can follow us back to the ranch—that is, if you don't have anything more important to do."

Matt liked both of his brothers-in-law. Jordan was the more serious member of the family, even if Kat had taken some of the starch out of him. Jeremy, on the other hand, was still the kid and always would be. Almost ten years younger than Jessie, he had been barely six months old when their mother had left them. He teased Jessie, made her laugh, aggravated her intentionally, and loved her deeply. No harm would ever come to Jessie if Jeremy were near.

Matt wanted to encourage him to spend time at the ranch with Jessie, especially if Matt had to be away. He took it for granted that Jeremy would have the opportunity.

No one in the family knew exactly what he did for a living, but he never seemed to be in need of money. He didn't spend lavishly. He traveled frequently, presumably on business. He didn't have a permanent address. He was now staying at Jessie's house in Spruce Creek since she'd moved up to the ranch. Before that, he had been living in the apartment above the clinic.

Matt was confident he could count on Jeremy.

FOURTEEN

MATT CONTINUED TO BE TROUBLED BY THE Ayers episode, so he put one or another of the ranch hands to riding the ridge line once or twice a week, looking for indications of trespassers.

"Let me know if there is any sign of intrusion," he told them.

After a few weeks when there had been no new incidences, life at the ranch returned to normal.

Pursuing his desire to diversify the livestock on the ranch, Matt acquired a green colt. His decision to train and sell quality saddle horses opened another aspect of ranching—one that would keep him personally involved. When he found an animal he believed had potential, he would buy it and bring it to the ranch to train himself. Well-trained horses were a good investment, and the activity kept Matt engaged. It wasn't as if he had no other work at the ranch, but getting away from keeping the ranch accounts cleared his head.

Additionally, he knew he was driving Jessica crazy when he was underfoot all the time. He worried about her, and he worried her with his constant concerns for her health. So, being out of the house with a project to complete kept everyone happy.

"Go away," she'd say. "Go do some ranch owner-stuff. Go count your goats or buy some cattle. Be a cowboy."

Matt didn't believe in *breaking* horses. His methods of training were geared toward building trust between himself and the animal. So, with that in mind, he had the colt turned into the corral between the barn and the house. He visited with the animal a couple of times a day, becoming a familiar and nonthreatening human. He occasionally brought the animal carrots, and eventually the colt trusted him enough to take the food from his hand.

Matt continued with gentling activities until the day came to place a saddle on the colt's back.

Jessie had come from the house to stand by

the fence and watch the activity. "When are you going to give that colt a name?" she asked her husband. "You can't just keep calling him 'colt'."

"Why not? If I name him Colt 45, then I can call him Colt forever. That will solve the naming problem."

"And if you breed him," Jessie said, "what will you call his offspring? Smith and Wesson?"

While they were bantering back and forth, Matt tied Colt loosely to the corral fence and slipped a saddle blanket onto his back. He had done this a few times before, and the animal didn't shy. Matt swung a saddle off the fence and onto Colt's back. He made no effort to cinch it, just let it sit with the straps atop the saddle bow. The horse did a couple of dance steps, widened his eyes, and swung his head around to look at the foreign burden on his back.

Matt's gentle voice soothed the animal. "Easy, boy. Get used to this weight. There's more to come, but this will do for today."

"You know, you'll be a wonderful father," Jessie mused.

"Are you suggesting I should raise a son the way I train a horse?" Matt asked.

"Our daughter could do a lot worse. You're patient and understanding. And while you *do* insist on getting your way, you go about enforcing your will in a gentle manner."

"Still not willing to concede we're having a boy?" Matt said.

"I'm not conceding anything until the day this baby is born."

Laughing at his wife, he took the lead rope and walked Colt about the corral. Matt would perform this same activity a couple of times a day for the next few until Colt was completely at ease with the saddle. Then he would fasten it loosely for a few days, and finally cinch it tight enough to take a man's weight.

Gentling a horse and gentling a wife had a lot in common, Matt thought. Take your time, do all in your power to make the horse and the woman feel loved and safe, but let them know you are in charge. Jessie would not appreciate being compared to a horse. But both were spirited creatures who required gentle handling.

After putting the tack away, Matt walked with Jessie back to the house. Consuela met them at the door to let them know lunch was ready.

JESSIE WAS LOOKING FORWARD TO THE BIG celebration in her brother's remodeled house. An unbroken tradition in the Walker clan since Jordan returned to practice in Spruce Creek, holiday gatherings were always held at his place. Even before he and Kat had married, Jordan had hosted Thanksgiving dinner.

The previous Thanksgiving, Jessie had been in New York and had missed the family celebration. But Matt had been there. That was the last year Jordan lived in the apartment above the clinic. Kat had been living there as well. Kat's brother Tony had joined Jeremy and Torrey as part of the family gathering.

Matt had told her that, thanks to Jeremy's heckling, Thanksgiving Day was when the family had learned of Jordan's and Kat's relationship. Apparently, it wasn't long after that day when Jordan decided he might want a more permanent arrangement.

Jeremy had been staying in the derelict family house across the road. Work had immediately commenced, converting the desperate structure into a warm and welcoming house and home. Jessie didn't know all the details, but when Jordan and Kat married in January, the house had been ready for them to occupy.

Jessie didn't have any warm childhood memories of living there. She wasn't certain how she would react to having all of her family in that place where only stress and sadness had existed when she was young.

She and Matt walked through the front door with Torrey and were enveloped by warmth and welcome. Kat had filled the house with homey personal touches. Sprays of autumn leaves bracketed the fireplace and a basket of gourds graced an end table placed next to a comfortable chair. The two family cats, Brando and Calamity Jane, darted out to inspect the new arrivals. Kat followed right behind with her infant daughter in her arms.

"Oh, good, you're here," she greeted. "Please take Faith so I can help Jordan in the kitchen."

Jessie struggled free of her coat and reached for the three-month-old baby.

"Matt, you know your way around the house—bring Consuela's pies into the kitchen and put Jessie's coat in the guest room," Kat directed.

Jessie laughed at the way Kat ordered her husband around. It was obvious they had become good friends while Jessie was back east.

"May Faith and I follow you into the kitchen

so we can chat while you work?" Jessie asked. Torrey had already moved in that direction.

"Well, you know how your brother is when he's cooking. But if you settle into a corner where he won't think you're underfoot, I think you'll be safe."

Jessie followed Kat into the kitchen, amazed at the changes. The kitchen was bright and cheerful, equipped with top-of-the-line modern appliances, and smelled wonderful. The turkey had obviously been in the oven for a while.

Torrey assumed responsibility for setting the dining room table. With Kat's family, there would be nine for dinner. She got to work right away.

"What's it like having a baby to take care of?" Jessie asked Kat.

"She's a good infant," Kat answered. "I take her to the clinic with me and it's much like having a small puppy to look after. But she doesn't get into things the way a pup would—at least, not yet."

Jessie snuggled the sweet-smelling bundle in her arms. Maybe having a baby wouldn't be a bad thing. She still had four months to go.

Jeremy arrived, followed shortly by Kat's brother Tony and her parents. They all congregated in the kitchen until Jordan had enough of their distraction.

"Go," he ordered, "watch football and sample the appetizers. Take the cats with you."

The game between Detroit and Houston was on, but no one watched intensely. Conversation took precedence over viewing a game where the outcome was unimportant. If the Broncos had been playing, the attention to the game would have been different.

Finally, after locking the cats away, they all settled at the dining room table. After grace, they dug into the turkey with all the trimmings.

Jessie admitted silently that it was good to be back among family. Her husband was going the extra mile to make her happy, and living at the ranch was no longer a bad thing.

MATT WAS GRATEFUL THE SNOW HAD STOPPED. While the afternoon was cold and the wind was blowing the fallen snow, the drive down to Spruce Creek for the Christmas Eve gathering at the Walker house would not be troublesome.

"Are you ready, Jess? I've brought the car around and the gifts are loaded."

"Coming."

Matt helped Jessie down the porch stairs to the waiting vehicle. He supported her until she settled into the passenger seat and stretched the belt across her lap below her belly. Then they were on their way.

What a difference from the previous year. Jessie had been away and he'd spent Christmas alone. He'd barely known the day had come and gone. There'd been no tree in his living room, no presents, no wife with whom to share love and joy.

"Matt," Jessie said, getting his attention. "I hate to admit it, but you were right."

"I usually am," Matt replied. "But what exactly am I right about this time?"

"We didn't have irreconcilable differences, we only had difficult choices. Thanks to your patience and the efforts, you made to make the ranch accessible, our choices were simplified. I won't be seeking a divorce."

Matt stopped the Rover so he could direct all his attention to Jessie. "Every effort, every penny spent was worth it if I brought you happiness." In a serious voice he continued, "That's all I ever wanted for you. I'm sorry I was so blind to your needs, and that I took you for granted."

He leaned across the console, took her face

in his hands, and kissed her gently. "You know, you've just given me the best Christmas gift ever," he whispered.

Jessie grinned at him. Then he knew that the high school girl he'd fallen in love with and who'd fallen in love with him had grown into this wonderful woman who was his wife, and soon-to-be the mother of his child. A man could not ask for more.

He started driving again, feeling relieved of a tremendous weight. If he were younger and of a less serious mien, he would whoop and holler. But he would content himself instead with a feeling of wonder and gratitude.

They stopped on their way to collect Torrey so she wouldn't be required to drive in case the weather turned nasty.

"You two look happy," Torrey remarked as Matt helped her into the car.

"Oh, we are," Matt replied.

He watched Torrey nod in satisfaction. He knew she was weighing the results of her instructions to him last April. "So, all is well?"

"It is."

"Hey, what are you guys whispering about back there?" Jessie called out in question.

"Christmas gifts," Matt replied.

"Well, let's get on our way. I want to see my niece."

When they arrived at the house, Jeremy had already appeared. Faith was in her activity center, bouncing with enthusiasm, and the cats were front and center, demanding their share of attention. Controlled chaos, Matt thought.

He greeted his brothers-in-law with manly hugs and kissed Kat on the cheek. Jessie had already plucked Faith from her play area, settled into a chair, and blew bubbles onto the baby's belly. Faith laughed gleefully.

Matt was convinced that, in spite of her fears, Jessie would be a wonderful mother.

"Well, Bro," Jeremy said, "my sister is looking very domesticated. You must be doing something right."

"Hush, Jeremy," Jordan hissed. "Jessie looks truly happy and content. But if we make an issue of it, she'll mutiny. Don't stir up trouble."

Matt agreed. "Jordan is right. Please, Jeremy, don't rock the boat. I wouldn't want our hard-won reconciliation destroyed by careless words."

"Sorry," Jeremy said. "Sometimes I forget not everyone appreciates my observations."

Torrey joined the group as Kat asked softly, "You *are* reconciled, then?"

Matt nodded. "On the way here she told me she won't be asking for a divorce. So, I'm convinced we are reconciled. Now I just need to keep her happy so she doesn't change her mind."

"Oh, surely she won't once the baby comes," Kat said.

Then, before any more furtive conversation could occur, Kat's family arrived. Tony and their parents hurried into the house and out of the cold. Bridget, Kat's mother, joined Jessie to coddle the little girl. Jessie surrendered the baby and her chair.

Matt mused as he looked around. *This is the future I want. Family and friends bonded together.*

FIFTEEN

After the Christmas Eve gathering at Jordan's house, Jessie and Matt spent a quiet Christmas Day together at the ranch. Most of the employees had been encouraged to take the week off to spend with family. Consuela was with her sister in Bailey. One of the ranch hands who had taken time off would drive her back when he returned.

Jessie would have been content to spend a second day cozied up with Matt and no one else around. But that was not to be. While it was the day after Christmas, she had an appointment with her obstetrician, so they would be driving down the mountain.

Jessie wanted her exam to go well. She knew she'd gained weight and hoped that meant the baby is growing. It had been a month since her last visit and, other than a backache, she'd not experienced a great deal of discomfort.

When they arrived at the doctor's office, Matt helped her from the car and kept a hand under her elbow because the pavement was icy in places. In the office, the nurse escorted her into the examining room and helped her undress and settle onto the exam table. Then Matt came in and joined her.

After the exam, Dr. Graham asked them to come into her office.

"Are there problems?" Jessie asked. Matt sat next to her holding her hand.

Dr. Graham nodded. "I'm afraid there are. Your cervix is relaxing which almost guarantees a premature birth. You are twenty-five weeks along. A baby now will have only a fifty percent chance of survival."

Jessie tensed. Maybe she hadn't wanted this baby in the beginning, but she did now.

"What can we do?" Matt asked.

"There is a procedure called Shirodkar cerclage, which in layman's language involves stitching around the opening of the cervix to prevent it from dilating," Dr. Graham explained. "There are risks inherent in the procedure, which include causing premature labor. But without it I can almost guarantee Jessica will deliver very soon—too soon for a guaranteed good outcome."

Jessie and Matt looked at each other, fear written on their faces.

"I can do the procedure this afternoon. It's neither long nor difficult. I will want you to stay one night in the hospital to make certain there are no complications, though. Then you'll be allowed to return to the ranch."

Matt glanced at Jessie and nodded his agreement.

"When it's complete, Jessica," Dr. Graham continued, "you'll be confined to bed rest. Maybe when you come down to stay on Valentine's Day you'll be allowed some quiet time out of bed. But until then, you can only leave your bed to use the restroom. There will be no showers or baths. You will have your meals in bed. No intercourse or sexual stimulation. Can you agree to that?"

"I guess I have no choice," Jessie responded.

"It's either accepting complete bed rest at home, or being hospitalized for the next thirteen weeks."

"I'll stay in bed. I promise."

"Should I hire a nurse for her?" Matt asked.

"Only if there's no one else who can give her bed baths, wash her hair, and help her with her hygiene."

"I can do those things," Matt said.

"And I'm certain Kat would help," Jessie added.

"Good, it's decided, then," the doctor said with an approving nod.

Dr. Graham's nurse made arrangements with the hospital for an operating room and patient admission. Fortunately, since it was the day after Christmas, there weren't any elective surgeries scheduled so there was no problem securing an OR.

Matt drove the few short blocks to the hospital and got Jessie checked in.

She donned the unflattering hospital gown and settled onto the bed. It was late morning, but she wouldn't be offered anything to eat until after the procedure.

An anesthesiologist came in and asked a number of questions, most concerned with what foods she had consumed that morning. The woman seemed relieved Jessie had eaten lightly and, indeed, was already hungry again.

Another hospital employee arrived with a raft of papers requiring her signature. That person was followed by a lab technician who drew blood and then disappeared.

Matt appeared worried. "If this is such a simple procedure, why all the activity?"

"It's what hospitals do," Jessie replied. "If I'd come in for a hangnail it would be just the same."

Matt squeezed her hand. "You're being very brave."

Jessie squeezed back. "I'm confident everything will be just fine."

"I sure hope you're right. I don't want anything to happen to you."

MATT PACED THE SURGICAL WAITING ROOM. Everyone assured him the procedure was minimally invasive, almost never had complications, and was the best chance of extending Jessie's pregnancy until a viable delivery could occur.

While waiting for news, Matt called his brother-in-law at the clinic. Torrey told him Jordan was unable to talk because he was treating an injured animal. "Kat's free if you want to talk to her."

"No, you're closest to Jess. Let me tell you

what's happening, and you can share with Jordan and Jeremy if he's around."

"Is something wrong?" Torrey asked.

"Jess had a follow-up appointment with the obstetrician this morning. Apparently, her cervix is beginning to relax and the OB is concerned she'll go into premature labor. Right now, she's in the OR. They're doing a procedure called a Shirodkar cerclage."

"A what?"

"A Shirodkar cerclage. The procedure involves sewing the opening of the cervix closed so it can't dilate."

"That sounds dreadful."

"The worst part is that, after it's completed and Jess comes home, she'll be on bed rest at least until we come down to stay in mid-February. She's going to be a beast to live with . . . wait, the doctor's coming."

"Mr. Whitaker, Jessica's doing fine. She's in recovery, shaking off the residual anesthesia. She'll be moved to a room in the maternity wing very soon. I'll be by this evening to see how she's doing and, of course, in the morning to discharge her."

"Thank you, Doctor," Matt replied as she departed.

Turning back to his iPhone, he asked Torrey how much she had heard.

"Enough to know everything went well and the two of you plan on returning tomorrow. I'll give Jordan the details, and I'm certain we'll be at the ranch in the next day or two."

"Give us a day to settle in. Come up on Friday or Saturday."

"Okay, will do. Give Jess our love. And hang in there, Matt. Everything will be fine."

Matt broke the connection and found an elevator to the birthing center. He went to the nurses' station and inquired about Jessie's room and anticipated arrival. The nurse was very calm and helpful. She directed Matt to his wife's room and told him he could wait there; that she would be brought up very soon.

Matt looked around when he entered. This room was not like the birthing suite they'd seen when they'd toured the maternity facilities. This was a very normal hospital room with nothing to distinguish it. There was no bassinet, nor was the bed a birthing bed. And the visitor chair was not the recliner intended for the father's overnight stay. This hospital room obviously was designed for prenatal hospitalization, and close to the birthing center should it be needed.

While he thought about what would probably be an uncomfortable night sitting up with Jessie, he heard the door open and watched the attendant push a gurney into the room. Jessie was awake, but not exactly perky.

A nurse hustled into the room. "Will you please wait in the hall, Mr. Whitaker, until we can get your wife settled into bed?"

He would have preferred to stay, but figured he wouldn't win the argument, and would only upset Jessie. So he meekly left the room and stationed himself outside the closed door.

Very little time passed before he was once again admitted to his wife's side. Jessie looked tired but not unwell.

"How do you feel?" he asked.

"I'll live. I'm just a little groggy. I don't hurt or anything. I'm hungry."

"Let me see what I can do to cure that. I'm not much good at curing most things, but I think I can get you some food."

Stepping out to the nurses' station, he asked if Jessie could have something to eat. He was assured she could and would.

Returning to her room, he said, "Mission accomplished. You'll get something to eat very shortly. Apparently, your request isn't uncommon since most patients go into the OR on an empty stomach."

Matt pulled the visitor chair up next to Jessie's bed. "I called the clinic to let Jordan know what's happening. He was unavailable, but I talked to Torrey. I gave her what details I knew. I was still on the phone when Dr. Graham came out of the OR and gave me the update. So, Torrey heard everything I did. I told her not to let them come to the ranch before Friday or Saturday."

"You're a great patient advocate. I'm glad I decided to keep you around."

"I am too. I can't tell you how much it means to me that you and I are a couple and will stay that way no matter what happens."

JESSIE WAS GRATEFUL TO BE AT HOME IN HER own bed. She'd not been comfortable in the hospital, even though Matt had stayed with her.

She had seven weeks of bed rest ahead before she moved down to Lakewood to wait out the final six weeks of her pregnancy. She knew she would get progressively more and more restive as the time passed. She loved to read, but she couldn't do it sixteen hours a day, seven days a week, for the next forty-eight days. She anticipated that, by the end of that time, she would come to hate her bed.

When he joined her in the bedroom, Matt told her that he'd hired a nurse to take care of her. "A nurse can see to all your needs. She'll bathe you and give you massages. She can help you to the bathroom. You won't need to worry about a thing. And your family won't need to make the drive up here too often. She'll start tomorrow."

"Matt, stop right now. You can't be making decisions for me. I need to be consulted. Just because I'm pregnant doesn't mean you can run my life. I am still my own person. I can take care of myself and my baby."

"He's my baby too. And I *will* make decisions for his welfare," Matt said.

"Your controlling behavior is one of the reasons I'd planned to divorce you," Jessie snapped back. "All that time you were courting me you were sweet as pie, and now your true colors are showing again."

"Planned to divorce me? I didn't know you'd reached a decision. All this time I thought we were working things out," Matt snarled. "What about your announcement Christmas Eve? A couple of nights ago you told me there would be no divorce. Are you taking that back?"

"I think I probably will. I wouldn't be the first woman to raise a child alone."

"That boy is my son, and he will grow up on this ranch."

"My daughter will stay with her mother." Jessie was in tears. She hated being so emotional, but Matt had crossed the line and her anger knew no bounds. "Please leave, and don't bring me any nurse. I won't have a stranger here."

The truth hit her hard—Matt hadn't changed. He was just as pig-headed and controlling as ever. And she was in no position to do anything about it.

The next morning there was no nurse, but Matt's behavior toward Jessie was stiff and formal. "What can I do to make you more comfortable?" he asked. "Would you like your laptop in here so you can watch movies online?"

"Sure. I'd also like a tilt-top table I can use in bed. Maybe I could do one of those thousand-piece jigsaw puzzles. When you bring me my laptop, I'll look online and see what I can find."

She would be prohibited from any real design work. At most, she could do some conceptual sketches while lying in bed. She could use the Internet to stay in touch with some of her clients. At least they wouldn't think she'd dropped off the face of the earth.

On Saturday her whole family descended on her. She was happy to see them and enjoyed the distraction.

Jeremy brought her an iPad filled with games. "You can take out some of your frustration blowing up *Chicken Invaders*," he told her. "If it doesn't relieve some aggressive tendencies, it will at least make you laugh."

Jessie hugged her brother, tears in her eyes.

"Hey, Sis, are you okay?"

"I'm fine, Jeremy. The tears are just baby hormones." Jessie grinned. "Only you would think of bringing me *Chicken Invaders*."

"Move over, Jerm, let me give Jessie a hug too." Jordan leaned in, ignoring his little brother's scowl. "I didn't bring you any gifts except my daughter to entertain you." Jordan took Faith from his wife and handed her to Jessie. The baby immediately started chortling and pulling on Jessie's hair.

Kat retrieved her daughter long enough for Torrey to hand Jessie a gaily wrapped package. Tearing it open, Jessie found a soft bed jacket.

"Torrey, thank you. This will dress up the appearance of the over-sized T-shirts I sleep in and will keep my shoulders warm. You always know what's exactly right."

"That's my job," Torrey said. "Have you had a bed-bath since you've been home?"

"Not yet. Matt's been busy. He tries, but he's not the world's greatest nurse."

"Then," Torrey said, "let's shoo the men out and clean you up. You'll feel like a new person."

The three men left with Faith, and the two women set to work.

Torrey had brought the appropriate supplies: dry shampoo, body wash that didn't require rinsing, moisturizing cream, and other toiletries designed for the bed-bound. When Jessie was clean and refreshed, clothes changed, and hair brushed, Kat and Torrey replaced the sheets on the king-sized bed with Jessie still in it.

"Wow, thanks. I feel like a new person," Jessie said. "But that was quite a workout. Even Muffin enjoyed the exercise. She's kicking up a storm."

It was true—the unborn infant's movement was visible beneath Jessie's distended belly.

"When did you start calling the baby Muffin?" Torrey asked. "And why?"

"I got tired of referring to my unborn child as *it*, and the saying 'a bun in the oven' prompted me to call her Muffin."

The women were chuckling when the men returned, and Faith reached for her mother.

"I think she's hungry," Jordan said.

Kat settled into a chair near the bed, covered herself for modesty, and put Faith to the breast. Matt looked a little uncomfortable, but Jessie's two brothers didn't act the least bit bothered.

"How long do you plan to keep breast feeding?" Jessie asked.

"At least another month or two," Kat said. "How about you, are you planning to nurse?"

"I haven't given it a lot of thought. Since I still have three months to go. I've just been focusing on getting there. I'd like to nurse, if I can. I think it strengthens the bond between mother and child," Jessie said. "Perhaps if my mother had nursed her children she wouldn't have just walked out on us." There was a decided bitterness to the last statement.

Jeremy jumped in with the apparent intention of lightening the tense atmosphere. "All this talk of boobs is making us men uncomfortable. Let's change the subject."

"Jeremy Walker, when did talk of boobs ever

make you uncomfortable?" Torrey challenged. "I've watched you ogle plenty of them."

Everyone laughed and the mood immediately relaxed.

Later, as they prepared to make the trek back down to Spruce Creek, Torrey said to Jessie, "Weather allowing, Kat and I will be back on Wednesday."

"Are you certain?" Jessie asked. "You don't mind the drive?"

"Not at all. We'll see you then."

SIXTEEN

JESSIE WOKE WITH AN ACHING BACK. SHE TRIED turning over—which, with her big belly, wasn't easy—but even resting on her side did not lessen the painful discomfort. She was grateful she only had another two months. If she wasn't released from the prison of bed-rest in the near future she would go mad.

Her doctor had promised once she relocated to Lakewood, nearer the hospital, Jessie would be allowed mild exercise. She would be allowed simple things like being permitted to sit at a table for meals and to walk around in the little house Matt had rented for their stay. In two weeks they would leave the ranch and quietly celebrate Valentine's Day in the rental. And then wait out the last six weeks.

Consuela entered the bedroom carrying a breakfast tray—the aroma of bacon invaded the room. Jessie sealed her lips to avoid gagging and insulting Consuela's cooking. She just couldn't face food this morning.

"Consuela, no breakfast for me this morning. I don't feel like eating."

"*Señora*, are you sick? Should I get *Señor* Matt?"

"No, I'm just not hungry. Maybe I'll eat later."

As Consuela left muttering to herself in Spanish, Jessie tried again to find a comfortable position that would relieve her back pain. The baby must be uncomfortable as well. Muffin was turning and kicking Jessie in the kidneys. With the last kick, Jessie knew she needed to make her way to the bathroom. The pressure was unbearable.

When she pulled herself up from the bed a flood of liquid gushed from her body. Embarrassed, thinking she had failed to make it to the bathroom in time, she realized her water had broken. Now her backache made sense. She was going into labor.

She fell back onto the bed and yelled out to Consuela.

"Hurry, call Matt. I need him," she panted.

"*Sí Señora*, I will get him *pronto*."

Consuela rushed out and soon Jessie heard the big bell on the porch clanging its peal for help. She knew there were things she should be doing, but weak as she was from a month spent in bed and clumsy from her misshapen body, she feared any attempt to get ready for the trip to the hospital would do more harm than good. So she gritted her teeth and waited.

After the clamor of the bell quieted, Consuela rushed back into the bedroom. "*Señor Matt* will hear the bell and will come soon." Then she went to the closet and pulled out a small suitcase. Even though it was months before they anticipated needing it, the case had been packed ready with essentials.

"Consuela, I must change clothes. I can't go anywhere in wet garments. I need warm clothes."

Consuela pulled a long heavy flannel nightgown from the bureau. After helping Jessie into the clean nightie, Consuela pulled out a heavy wool robe and wrapped Jessie warmly. She was gathering boots and socks when Matt rushed into the room.

"What's wrong? Why was the bell ringing?"

"My water broke," Jessie answered. "We need to get to the hospital."

"Did you call the doctor?"

"No, it happened so suddenly, I've not had time."

Matt pulled out his cell phone and punched a single number. He had the doctor on speed dial. He put the call on speaker phone. When he reached her service, he quickly told the operator what was happening. Before he could begin providing details, the doctor's voice was on the line.

"Start out immediately. I will send an ambulance to meet you en route. Drive carefully, but don't delay."

"Thank you, Dr. Graham. We're on our way," Matt said before breaking the connection.

Consuela had pulled socks onto Jessie's feet and was starting to put on her boots.

"Don't bother," Matt said, "I'll carry her."

For the first time ever, Consuela argued with her employer. "She needs boots. Her feet will be cold."

Jessie was amused Matt was taken aback by Consuela's challenge. But Jessie was glad Consuela spoke up. Jessie still trembled with fear, but now that Matt was with her everything would be all right.

MATT WAS SHAKEN BUT REFUSED TO LET IT show. Jessica depended on him to be her shelter in a storm, and he wasn't going to let her down. He was concerned for the child, of course, but his priority was Jessie. Nothing could be allowed to happen to her.

He feared all the work he had done to bring their marriage back into harmony may have been destroyed by their fight in December. Jessie had been cool and distant toward him for the past month. There'd been no further talk of divorce, but there'd not been reconciliation either.

He brought the Range Rover to the front of the ranch house. He confirmed the fuel tank was full. The heater was going full on, and by the time he got Jessie into the vehicle, the chill would have vanished.

Jessie was ready in heavy robe over her nightgown and boots and socks on her feet. Wool mittens covered her hands and a warm scarf protected her ears. Consuela also wore her coat and gloves. She carried an assortment of pillows and blankets.

"I go too, *Señor* Matt. The *Señora* needs a woman."

Matt decided there was no point in arguing. He picked Jessie up into his arms and motioned

Consuela to follow them out.

When he started to put Jessie in the front seat, Consuela told him to lay her in the back seat. "I will ride with her, keep her safe."

The housekeeper arranged pillows against the back door. Matt laid Jessie down on the bench seat and Consuela covered her with a blanket. Then she slid into place and put Jessie's feet in her lap.

There was no way to put a seat belt around Jessie, so Matt would simply have to drive fast and careful. Consuela put the extra blankets and pillows on the back floorboard between Jessie and the back of the driver's seat. If her shoulders slid she would be buffered.

He engaged the four-wheel drive and started down the ranch road to the highway. Once again, he gave thanks the road had been leveled and graveled. Even the rigors of a hard winter had not noticeably disturbed the surface. He was able to maintain a steady thirty miles an hour. On the highway he pushed up to fifty-five. He would like to travel faster, but it was barely dawn and dark patches of the highway could easily hide black ice.

He tried to focus on his driving, but he could hear an occasional groan from the back of the car. "Jess, are you okay?"

"The *Señora* is having labor. Not hard, not fast, but it starts."

When they reached a point where Matt thought they might have a cell signal, he engaged the Bluetooth to call his brother-in-law. When he connected to the clinic, he told Torrey they were on their way to the hospital in Lakewood. He didn't have time to say much more before they were out of range again. He knew Torrey would pass the word.

Matt's mind kept diverting to concerns for Jessie's well-being. It was necessary for the cervical cerclage to be reversed before the baby started to come. *Would an EMT be able to remove the stitches so Jess wouldn't tear? What about their baby? Could an infant survive arriving this early? If they lost the infant, would Jess be able to cope?* She'd not wanted to get pregnant, but once she discovered she was carrying their child, she'd devoted herself to doing everything right. He couldn't let her blame herself if the worst happened.

Matt was grateful the traffic down the mountain was light. He chewed his lip when he got behind a slow moving vehicle and was forced to wait for a safe place to pass.

They'd been on the road forty-five minutes when Matt heard the sound of a siren approaching. He turned on his high beams and began blinking his headlights on and off. The ambulance slowed as it approached the Range Rover and returned the signal. Matt pulled onto the shoulder of the highway and waited.

The ambulance turned on its flashing blue lights and made a U-turn in the middle of the highway. The driver pulled the vehicle in front of Matt and the EMTs jumped out and approached—the driver, a big muscular black man, the other, a petite redhead who resembled his sister-in-law.

"Boy, I'm glad to see you," Matt said lowering the windows. "My wife's in the back seat. Her name is Jessica."

The EMTs pulled a gurney from the back of the ambulance and approached the back door that Jessie rested against. "Jessica, can you hear me?" the driver asked.

"Yes," she responded weakly.

"We are going to open the door supporting you. We will do it slowly and hold your body weight so you won't fall. Then we will move you onto the gurney and put you in the ambulance. Red here," he said, motioning to the other EMT, "will ride in the back with you."

"Okay," Jessie said.

The redheaded EMT spoke to Matt. "Has she begun having contractions?"

Matt looked to Consuela who answered, "Sí, far apart and not hard yet."

Matt spoke up and added, "She had a cervical cerclage procedure. She needs the stitches removed."

"I can do that if it becomes necessary, but we would rather wait and let the doctor do the reversal in the hospital."

Matt nodded.

"Follow us, but don't try to keep up. We'll be driving carefully, but there are places where we can safely drive faster than the speed limit allows." The petite woman moved to the gurney and the two EMTs lifted Jessie into the back of the ambulance. Then she jumped in as well.

In spite of their size difference they worked well together as a team, Matt thought.

Consuela moved to the front seat and they drove off behind the ambulance with its flashing blue lights, siren silent.

THE EMTS HAD LOCKED THE GURNEY IN PLACE and secured Jessie with straps across her body. She felt physically safe for the moment, but terrified of what was to come.

"My name is Ginger," the female EMT introduced herself. "Our driver is Rafe. He is the best ambulance driver in Colorado."

"Thank you for being here. I'm so scared."

"Is this your first child?"

"Yes, but Muffin isn't due for two months yet. I'm very early."

"Muffin, is that the baby's name?"

"Not really. It is just what Matt and I call it. You know 'a bun in the oven'."

"Cute," Ginger laughed, squeezing Jessie's hand gently.

"First babies take their time being delivered. I know. I've had two," Ginger added. "We will have you in the hospital in plenty of time. And you and your baby will be well taken care of. Now do your best to relax."

The forty-minute ambulance ride to the hospital was mostly uneventful. Jessie did experience two contractions about twenty minutes apart, but Ginger seemed unconcerned so Jessie relaxed and tried to ignore the worsening backache.

When they reached the hospital, an orderly wheeled Jessie to a birthing suite where a nurse helped her to undress and don a hospital gown. She'd just barely settled onto the delivery bed when Dr. Graham appeared.

"Okay, my dear, let's get the stitches undone so nature can take its course."

After reversing the procedure accomplished just a month earlier, the doctor checked the level of dilation. The Shirodkar had prevented the cervix from expanding, but now with the cerclage removed, labor would proceed more quickly.

"What about the baby?" Jessie asked. "Will she survive?"

"Your four weeks of bed rest have increased the chance of survival from fifty percent to over ninety percent. You can relax. The baby should be fine."

"Thank God. Please let Matt know when he gets here. He was as worried as I."

"He's already here getting your admission paperwork completed. But I'll speak with him," the doctor assured her.

A nurse came into the room as the doctor was leaving. "Hi, I'm Ann, your nurse. I'm going to attach an EFM to your belly," she told Jessie. "It'll keep track of the baby's heartbeat and accurately measure your contractions. It's a normal procedure we do for every delivery."

"I remember being told about fetal monitoring when we did our hospital tour. No wires, right?"

"Correct, it's done by telemetry so you can move around to stay comfortable. You can even get up and walk around as long as someone is with you."

"You have no idea how good that statement makes me feel. I have been on bed rest for the past four weeks. I can't wait to get up and walk around."

Just at that moment a contraction struck and Jessie moaned. "Between contractions that is."

Once the monitor was attached, Ann helped Jessie from the bed. She was weak because of her forced inactivity but was able to stand without assistance and walk across the room. She stretched her arms and tried to straighten her back. The small amount of exercise relaxed her.

When Matt walked into her room he exclaimed, "What are you doing out of bed?"

The nurse intervened. "Hi, I'm Ann, your wife's nurse. Once labor has started bed rest is no longer necessary, nor even desired. As long as there is someone with her to prevent a fall, standing and walking are productive activities."

"Oh, okay."

Jessie watched Matt with amusement. Now with her own concerns addressed, she felt relaxed and only a little apprehensive.

Nodding at Matt the nurse said, "If you're prepared to assume your paternal attendant duties, I'll return to the desk and leave you in privacy, but no monkey business." The nurse gave him a smug grin. "I can see the monitor output at the nurses' station, so I'll know how she's doing without intruding."

"Thank you, Ann," Jessie said. "I'll ring if I need you. I don't suppose you can tell me how long labor will last."

"I can say with assurance labor will last as long as it lasts—that is until your baby is ready to be born. Your pains are still at twenty minutes apart and relatively mild so you have a while to go."

After Ann left, Jessie turned to Matt. "Are you okay? You seem stressed."

Matt encircled Jessie in an embrace. "Of course I'm stressed. My wife is in premature labor and I'm worried about her and my child."

SEVENTEEN

MATT WAS CONCERNED FOR JESSIE, BUT HE WAS bored doing nothing but sitting around. She'd been here twenty-four hours, and if her water hadn't broken, they could be waiting at home. Well, maybe not at home. That was farther away from the hospital than either of them would want to be, but they could be waiting somewhere less institutional.

"Jess," he said, "would you like to be alone for a while? I get the feeling that me being here pacing like a caged lion is making you uncomfortable. The hospital can call me if something starts happening."

"Thank you, Matt. You're so intuitive. I didn't want to tell you to go away, but I would like some solitude," she admitted. "There's a lot you can be doing while I'm waiting."

"Like what?"

"Have you phoned my brothers?"

"Jeremy is in Switzerland or somewhere in Europe. But I can call Jordan."

"And we need somewhere to stay after I'm discharged. The baby will need to stay in the hospital for a while. We won't need the house, but maybe a bed and breakfast close to the hospital."

"Right, I'll cancel the house and find us a B&B."

"What about Consuela? I feel terrible. I never asked what happened to her after I was transferred to the ambulance. She's not sitting in the waiting room, is she?"

Matt smiled. He felt as if his old Jessica was back. She was in the hospital but worried about their housekeeper.

"Once I was certain you were being admitted, I called Hank to come pick her up. She was home less than four hours after our wild ride."

"I'm glad you were looking out for her. Even if I was distracted, I should have asked about her sooner. I'm so grateful she rode with me."

"So am I."

Matt kissed Jessie on the forehead and left

the birthing suite. Except to use the men's room, he hadn't been out of Jessie's presence since he was first allowed to be with her. Now, with projects to complete, he felt useful.

He drove the Rover out of the hospital parking lot and went in search of a coffee shop. He found Panera Bread east of the hospital on South Wadsworth. His timing was good. It was late enough he'd missed the early morning rush and early enough he was there before the lunch crowd.

He dispensed a cup of real coffee from the urn of dark roast. He knew why hospitals didn't serve regular coffee to their patients, but it seemed cruel to inflict only decaf on visitors. The lack of caffeine in his system probably contributed to his anxieties.

He opened his iPhone to search for a B&B near the hospital. He was surprised to learn the nearest were back up in the foothills. So then he looked for alternatives. Nearby, to the east of the hospital, he found a Homewood Suites hotel. He decided to check it out.

When he arrived at the hotel, he observed the exterior. The grounds were clean and well maintained. At the desk he asked to speak with the manager. When she arrived, she guided Matt to a comfortable seating area in the lobby.

"Good morning. I'm Lynnette Longfield, the manager on duty. How can I help you?"

"My wife is in the hospital at St. Anthony's. She's in premature labor."

"Oh, I'm sorry," the woman interjected.

"We live on a ranch in the mountains ten miles west of Bailey," Matt continued. "Since the baby will need to remain in the hospital, we want somewhere to stay that is close to St. Anthony's. Your hotel seems to match my criteria for location."

"I think you'll find our facility very comfortable, as well," Lynnette said. "I'm assuming you're looking for an extended stay?"

"Maybe as much as a month."

She brought out a hand-held gadget and began asking questions. "Smoking or non-smoking?"

"Non-smoking," Matt said emphatically.

"One or two bedrooms?"

"One."

"One or two beds?"

"Two. She'll be recovering from the birth of the baby."

Lynnette smiled at him. "You are a very considerate husband. When do you think you will want to occupy the suite?"

"Today," Matt said. "This location is so close, I can be at the hospital in minutes if Jessica decides to have this baby tonight."

"Okay, you have a confirmed reservation for a one-bedroom suite, two queen-size beds, non-smoking, beginning today for the next four weeks." She took his credit card to guarantee for late arrival in the event he was delayed at the hospital.

"You can, of course, leave before the end of that period with no extra charges, provided you give us forty-eight-hours notice. And you may check in this afternoon after three."

Matt breathed a sigh of relief. What had appeared to be the biggest task had been relatively easy to accomplish. It was done now, and he could focus on Jessie and the baby. And, if for some reason the rooms proved unsatisfactory, he had plenty of time to make a change before Jessie was released from the hospital.

He wandered into the hotel restaurant which was open for lunch. After ordering his meal, he pulled out his iPhone and called the clinic. He kept his voice low. He'd always disapproved of people talking loudly on cell phones in public places, especially in restaurants.

"Hi, Torrey, is Jordan available?"

"Yes. Just a minute. Is something wrong? You don't sound like yourself."

"Let me talk to Jordan. He can give you the details."

"Hey, Matt," Jordan greeted his brother-in-law. "What's up?"

"Jessie's water broke yesterday, and she's in the hospital in Lakewood in early labor. I didn't call sooner because nothing much seems to be happening. But if the activity level doesn't increase, the doctor intends to give Jess something to speed it up. So, if the baby doesn't come tonight, he'll certainly be born tomorrow."

"Let us know when that happens. Kat, Torrey, and I'll drive down to be at St. Anthony's when the time comes."

"Will do. How about Jeremy? Is there any way to contact him?"

"I don't know of one, but Torrey might."

Matt's meal was delivered. "I have to go, Bro. I'll keep in touch."

ANN CAME INTO JESSIE'S ROOM WEARING A BIG smile. "All alone, are you?" she asked.

"Matt was stressed, so I suggested he find us a place to stay after the baby is born. I needed to get him out of my hair," Jessie said with a grimace.

Ann took Jessie's hand. "It will soon be over. You'll be so happy when you hold your infant in your arms. Do you know the gender of the baby?"

"No, I wanted to be surprised. I want a girl. Matt wants a boy. But we'll both be delighted with whichever . . ." Jessie curled into herself and let out a loud cry as her belly contracted. "My pains are worse."

"Breathe slowly," Ann said as she counted the seconds of the contraction. She made a note on Jessie's patient chart. The EFM accomplished the same thing electronically.

"It hurts," Jessie whimpered.

"I know, child, I know." Ann squeezed her hand. "I'll let the doctor know your progress. She'll probably want to check you again."

Jessie assumed Dr. Graham had been in the hospital, because she appeared in the room in less than twenty minutes.

"Finally, your labor is progressing," she told

Jessie. "You're at eight centimeters. I think we can expect the baby in the next few hours."

"Can you give me something for the pain?"

"Not yet, I don't want to do anything that will slow the baby's progress. Where's your husband? I thought he would be here with you."

"He's out finding us a place to stay until the baby can go home. We need to call him and get him to come back."

"Relax, Jessica, I'll get your nurse to track him down. We still have plenty of time."

After Dr. Graham left, Jessie tried to doze, but labor pains jolted her awake. Finally, Matt was at her side.

"Where were you?" she cried. "I was afraid the baby would come, and you wouldn't be here."

"Hush, I'm here now. The doctor says you still have awhile to go." Matt squeezed her hand, and she gratefully accepted his reassurance.

"I've found us a place to stay until the baby can go home. There's an extended stay hotel close to the hospital. We'll be able to come back and forth any time we want."

"What about my brothers? Did you let them know what's happening?"

"I talked to Jordan. He said it's possible Torrey can reach Jeremy. Jordan and Kat will come down when it's time."

"You might want to let them know now," Jessie gasped. "I think Muffin is on her way."

Apparently, the EFM alerted Jessie's nurse to the same conclusion because she rushed into the room to manually check Jessica.

Matt stepped out and Jessie called after him, "Where are you going?"

"I'm calling your brother. I'll be right back."

Jessie gritted her teeth and endured another contraction. A relaxant was injected into her IV, and she sighed with relief. Soon all this pain would be over. But if they stayed married, Matt had better never think of getting her pregnant again.

She drifted into a twilight sleep. She felt Matt take her hand and stroke her forehead. Then another pain hit. She had no idea how long her ordeal lasted—too long, she was certain.

He told her to breathe, and then the doctor told her to push. Too many people were telling her what to do. Then, with one final heave, it was over. She heard her child cry out loud and strong.

The baby was in a portable incubator in her delivery room. He'd been put there as soon as the nurse had cleaned him. The pediatrician checked the child, and then approached the new parents.

"You have a beautiful baby boy. He's small—only two pounds thirteen ounces—but he seems healthy. We'll be moving him into neonatal intensive care, but I'm hopeful he won't develop any problems. He just needs to gain weight."

Jessie heard Matt thank the pediatrician. Then her husband leaned over and kissed her gently. "You did good, Mama."

Matt piled pillows at her back and helped her sit up. "Your family is here. Do you want to see them now? Or would you rather they wait?"

Jessie's nurse interrupted. "Let me get her cleaned up before she has visitors. Why don't you go give them the good news? I'll let you know when she's ready."

WHEN MATT ENTERED THE WAITING AREA, Jessie's brother almost tackled him. "How is she?" Jordan demanded.

"She's fine—exhausted—but she and the baby are both healthy. The nurse is cleaning her up now. Then you'll be able to see her briefly."

"Well, tell us, did she have a boy or a girl?" Torrey asked.

"We had a little boy," Matt said, bursting

with pride. "He weighed two pounds thirteen ounces, and if Jessie doesn't change her mind, we'll name him Thomas Michael."

Kat hugged her brother-in-law. "That's wonderful. But will the baby be okay? He's so small."

"The pediatrician was there during the delivery. He immediately checked little Thomas and told us as soon as the baby gains some weight, he'll be fine. Were you able to reach Jeremy?" Matt asked Torrey.

"I was able to leave a message for him after you called. He called back and wanted details. Since I had none to give him, I told him to call back tomorrow."

"Did he say where he was?"

"He told me he's in Zurich. I imagine he is on his way back to Colorado, even as we speak. He adores Jess and would want to be here for her."

As Matt was about to respond to Torrey, the nurse came into the waiting room and told Matt he could take Jessie's family in to see her.

"But don't let them stay too long," she warned.

Followed by his in-laws, Matt led the way back into the birthing suite. It was sad the bassinet near Jessie's bed was empty, but the knowledge their baby son was safely in the neonatal ICU took away some of the sense of disappointment.

"Hi, guys." Jessie looked radiant as she greeted her family.

Everyone started talking at once, all asking after her welfare. Matt absorbed the love in the room and prayed his son would grow up surrounded by this loving family. In spite of what Jessie might believe, he knew his wife was going to be a wonderful mother.

"Have any of you seen the baby yet?" Jessie asked, her voice carrying over the top of the conversational buzz.

When all the replies were in the negative, she urged them to find their way to the nursery to meet the newest member of the family.

"I need a moment with my husband, and then he'll join you."

As the family members dutifully filed out, Jessie reached out a hand to Matt.

"Are you okay?" he asked, feeling concerned.

"I'm fine. I just wanted a moment alone with you."

Matt's relief was palpable. "You have my undivided attention, Mrs. Whitaker."

"That's what I wanted to talk about. I intend to stay Mrs. Whitaker. I love you, and I love our son. We are family, and we will stay family."

"You have made me the happiest man in the world." Matt sighed. "I realize sometimes I'm overbearing. I'll work on that, I swear. If it's ever too much, just tell me to back down and I will. I love you, Jessica Walker Whitaker, and I will do everything in my power to be worthy of your love for me."

EPILOGUE

February, one year later...

HOSTING A BIRTHDAY PARTY AT THE RANCH IN February was not an option. Jessie was delighted when her sister-in-law had suggested Thomas celebrate his first birthday in the original Walker family home.

Since the house was different from what it had been during the difficult years of her youth, Jessie suffered no bitter memories when she entered. She basked in the warmth and love imbued in her surroundings. But she was only briefly allowed to enjoy the ambiance before chaos erupted.

When she came through the door, followed by her husband toting Thomas in his car-carrier, she was immediately grabbed around the legs by her tottering niece. Faith clutched at Jessie's knees and jabbered, "Up, up."

Helpless to do otherwise, she leaned down and raised Faith to her shoulder. "You know, little one," she said, sighing into her niece's ear, "you should allow Auntie to take off her coat before going in for a tackle." At eighteen months, the child was a force to be reckoned with.

The two cats circled Jessie's feet, adding to the confusion. Kat and Torrey came in from the kitchen. Kat took her daughter, allowing Jessie to get out of her winter coat. Torrey hugged Jessie and then turned to Matt and Thomas.

"Let me have that boy," Torrey demanded.

Matt handed the carrier over and removed his outer garments.

"Wow, you're getting heavy," Torrey teased the grinning infant.

"Dow, ow!" Thomas ordered. He couldn't quite say down or now, but his intention was clear. As soon as he was released from his carrier, he crawled to a nearby table and pulled himself up.

Thomas eyed the cats, as if contemplating going in chase, when he was diverted by his cousin grabbing and hugging him around the shoulders. "Tom-tom, Tom-tom," Faith chanted. They both abruptly sat on the floor, and Thomas seemed happy to be the center of his cousin's attention.

Jordan, Jeremy, and Jeremy's friend, Becky, arrived from the back of the house bearing wrapped gifts. Most were for Thomas, but there was a consolation gift or two for Faith.

They were piled in the corner of the room farthest from the blazing fire in the fireplace. Kat secured child-proof gates that would prevent either child from making a break into the kitchen or the hallway leading away from the living room. The cats had been banished for their own protection. The adults settled down to have a peaceful conversation, bringing everyone in the room up-to-date on everyone else's status.

The two children played contentedly, babbling with each other in a language only the two of them understood, until an unpleasant odor invaded the room.

The two mothers shared a grin. "They probably both need to be changed," Kat offered.

"Shall we let the men take charge?" Jessie asked with a smirk.

"Wonderful idea," Kat agreed.

"Gentlemen, your fathering skills are to be

tested and compared," she told her brother and her husband. "Let the competition begin."

Jordan and Matt groaned with good-natured complaint, but they picked up their children and headed off to the nursery.

"Jeremy, why don't you join them?" Jessie suggested. "Learn how it's done."

"You're just getting even with me for all my dirty diapers." Jeremy laughed, rising to his feet. "But that's okay. I'm safer with Matt and Jordan than I am with a room full of women."

"While they're gone, why don't we set up for the party?" Kat suggested.

"Sounds good to me," Torrey agreed.

The four women made their way together to the kitchen.

When the men and the children returned to the living room, a birthday cake with a single burning candle was held aloft by Jessie. "Matt, pick up Thomas and bring him close enough to blow out the flame."

"Me help?" Faith insisted.

"Sure." Matt nodded at Jordan. "Lift her up so she can blow out the candle too."

When the ritual was complete, the entire family retired to the dining room for cake and ice cream.

Jessie was overwhelmed with a sense of well-being. The premature infant who was so small at birth was now within normal parameters for height, weight, and development. Her marriage was stable. Her business was successful.

Who would believe an unwanted pregnancy would result in so much happiness?

I hope you enjoyed reading *Simply Provocative, A Spruce Creek Romance*. There is no greater satisfaction for an author than to know that her work is enjoyed by the reader. So if you enjoyed *Simply Provocative*, please tell others and consider posting a reader review online. Your word-of-mouth recommendation is the best reward you can give to any writer.

Jordan's and Kat's story is now available in *Simply Irresistible, A Spruce Creek Romance*, the first book in the series.

Watch for Jeremy's story appearing in *Simply Outrageous*, the next sweet romance of the Spruce Creek series.

ABOUT THE AUTHOR

Sharon Burgess was raised in San Francisco. She grew up immersed in all the exciting culture of the City by the Bay. Her mother's legacy to her was a love of reading, and Sharon had her first library card before age five.

She lived in Colorado for sixteen years and still owns property a few miles from the site of the fictional town of Spruce Creek.

Sharon wrote throughout her corporate career, but it was all boringly factual—staff reports, white papers, user manuals, advertising copy. In her leisure time, she read across all genres—fantasy, science fiction, westerns, mysteries. But she didn't discover romance until after her husband's death, when she read her first Nora Roberts love story.

"While my husband lived I didn't need to read romance," Sharon shares. "I had it in my life every day."

She is an active member of the California Writers Club Tri-Valley Branch and the San Francisco Area Chapter, Romance Writers of America.

When not at her computer writing or editing, Sharon is comfortably settled in her recliner with a cat in her lap and reading a romance novel.

Visit her website at www.SharonBurgess.com